Last Flight

A Last Healer Mystery

By Charles Huss

For my wife, Rose, who has always been my biggest fan.

Chapter 1

Steven North parked near his company's hangar well before sunrise. He took a deep breath and exhaled slowly. This was it. Today, he would know whether his company, which he poured his heart and soul into, not to mention all his money, would live or die.

He entered the code on the back door and went inside. The hangar felt cold, so he turned the thermostat up a few degrees. Heating such a large room was expensive, so he kept the temperature to a minimum when no one was there.

North, a tall and handsome man of forty-five, brewed himself a cup of coffee and reviewed his checklist. When he finished, he went to the bathroom. It would be his longest flight to date in his company's prototype aircraft, and it was critical that he reach his destination without any issues. He checked himself in the mirror. He adjusted his tie and combed his hair. He didn't like that his once thick, dark hair now had streaks of gray, but he had no desire to color it. Besides, he was happily married, and his wife thought the gray made him look distinguished.

He had never flown while wearing a suit before, at least not as the pilot, but he had an important meeting—very important. He pushed the button that opened the large hangar door and was greeted by a rush of cold air. He had taken off his coat, but it wasn't worth the trouble of putting it back on.

He grabbed a pull bar and walked to his airplane. It had been almost four years since he started his company, but less than three weeks had passed since the initial flight of their first aircraft. He hoped the company would survive long enough to mass-produce it.

He attached the pull bar and started to pull the aircraft out of the hangar when he heard a noise behind him. He turned and saw Sonia Wilson walking toward him. She was a beautiful, thirty-two-year-old woman of Hispanic descent. She wore a long white coat with its hood down, revealing her long, dark hair. It blew in the wind as she approached. When she got close enough, she said, "I just learned last night you filed a flight plan to Minneapolis. When were you going to tell me, Steve?"

Steve shook his head, set the pull bar down, and turned to Sonia. "I didn't tell you because I knew you would want to come along. Flying to Chicago is one thing, but Minneapolis is three hundred miles away."

"So? The aircraft is rated for three hundred and sixty miles."

"Technically, it hasn't been rated yet. Three hundred and sixty miles is a number the engineers came up with. It's just an estimate. We haven't tested its range in real-world flights yet. I figured this would be a great opportunity to prove what this aircraft can do."

"You mean you are sneaking off before sunrise to risk your life for an unnecessary test? Why don't you test it at two hundred miles first? If that goes well, you can try two hundred fifty and so on."

"I have my reasons."

"Reasons? What reasons can be worth such a risk?"

Steve sighed. "We don't have time for more tests."

"What do you mean we don't have time?"

"Look, Sonia. I didn't want to worry you, but the company is almost out of money. I'm meeting with a potential client today who runs a large flight training school. He's looking to buy at least ten planes to start, with plans for more in the future. If I can get a commitment from him, asking investors for more money will be much easier."

Sonia thought momentarily and asked, "How confident are you this plane will make it to Minneapolis?"

"I'm ninety-nine percent certain," Steve said. "If I'm wrong, I could probably put it down in a field or on a road somewhere."

Sonia thought momentarily and said, "Okay. I'm going with you."

"No, you are not. Even if the risk is only one percent, it's too high to take passengers."

"I'm not a passenger. I'm your Vice President of Sales. You need me there. I'm sorry to tell you this, Steve, but you're not a salesman. You're a great leader, but you can't sell. That's why you hired me."

"I hired you because you're the wife of my chief engineer, and he talked me into it. I kept you on and promoted you because you are smart and persuasive."

"Exactly," Sonia said. "That's why you need me there. Don't forget, most of your investors came through me. Selling to a flight school will be a piece of cake."

"I don't know, Sonia."

"Are we going to stand here and argue, or are we going to fly?"

North shook his head and said, "See what I mean about you being smart and persuasive? I hope I don't regret this."

Sonia smiled as Steve picked up the pull bar and continued to pull the aircraft out of the hangar. He then returned the pull bar, grabbed his coat, closed the main hangar door, and the two of them got into the aircraft.

No airplanes were flying in or out of the airport at that early hour, so they were able to taxi to the runway and take off without delay. Once they were in the air, the person watching them from a vehicle in the parking lot started the engine and drove away.

Sonia had flown with Steve in the same aircraft several days earlier when they flew to Chicago. She was surprised then how quickly they were in the air, and she was surprised again this time. She imagined it felt like taking off from an aircraft carrier.

After flying for almost an hour, Sonia turned to the right and saw a beautiful orange sky behind them. "I've never seen a sunrise from up here," she said. "It's quite beautiful."

"If we had the miles, I would circle so you could see it better."

"That's okay, Steve. I can see it just fine. It feels like heaven up here."

A loud bang from the back of the aircraft broke the serenity. The plane shook and pitched downward before leveling out. They both looked behind the seats, and Sonia said, "What the hell was that?"

"I don't know," Steve said, concern on his face. He looked at his instruments and saw their altitude slowly dropping. He tried the controls, but nothing happened. "I just lost all control of the aircraft."

Sonia's eyes widened, and her mouth fell open. "What? Are you sure?"

North tried every control at his disposal, but he could only control the plane's airspeed. That didn't help them. "I can't steer it," he finally said.

They were slowly descending, and there was nothing he could do to stop it. He saw ski slopes ahead of them. He needed lift to get over the peak, but everything was frozen. He cut their speed as much as possible without stalling. Just before impact, he turned to Sonia and said, "I'm sorry. I should have made you stay behind."

Chapter 2

"Good morning, Sunshine," Joe said as he entered the bedroom with a breakfast tray. "Happy birthday!"

Katie opened her eyes, looked out the window, and said, "You are very sweet, Joe, but it's still dark outside. Why are you up so early?"

"It's your birthday. It's a special day. Don't you want it to last as long as possible?"

"It would be even more special if I could sleep longer."

Joe set the tray on the nightstand and sat on the bed beside Katie. He kissed her and said, "I have a big day planned for you and want to start by watching the sunrise together."

Katie struggled to sit up in bed. Joe stood and helped her. He then put the tray of bacon and eggs with coffee on her lap. "I hope this baby comes soon," Katie said. "I don't think I can take much more of this."

"You and the baby are doing fine. It shouldn't be long now."

Katie took a bite of bacon and said, "So, where are we going to watch the sunrise?"

"I thought we could go to our favorite place."

"On top of the mountain? Are you crazy? Have you seen me lately? What if the baby wants to come while we are up there?"

"Finish your breakfast, and then we can connect to the baby and see if he's almost ready."

Katie loved to do that. As far as she knew, no other woman in the world could connect to their baby the way she could with Joe's help. "Okay, fine. You talked me into it."

When breakfast was over, Joe washed the dishes and sat next to Katie on the bed. They held hands, and Joe thought of Katie as an extension of himself.

Joe's gift allows him not only to sense what's happening inside his body but also to consciously direct his body to fight off invaders or repair any damage, including the effects of aging. Despite being over one hundred years old, he only recently discovered that he could extend his healing ability to others by touching them while mentally imagining they were an extension of his body.

4

LAST FLIGHT

Joe was born an orphan. His father was killed during the First World War. His mother was a refugee who died during childbirth the day her ship arrived in New York. He learned a year earlier, with Katie's help, that his family came from a small settlement in northwest Croatia that was decimated during the war when most of its male inhabitants died in the fighting. They also discovered that a Healer was born once or twice a century in that village. It was this increased awareness of his potential, combined with Katie on the brink of death, that allowed Joe to discover how to use his healing ability for others.

When Joe connected to Katie, it was as if they were one person. Katie could feel everything Joe felt. She could feel what was happening inside his internal organs as well as her own, the same way other people could feel their fingers and toes. Most importantly, they could both feel the baby. They knew more about the baby's health than any doctor could possibly know.

"Little Joey is perfectly happy where he is right now," Joe said.

"I wish I could tell him to hurry up."

"That would be nice, but I'm afraid it doesn't work that way."

Katie let go and said, "Okay. Help me get up so I can get ready."

"Really? You're not going to give me a hard time about this?"

"Of course not. I know you put a lot of thought into this day. I'm not going to ruin it for you."

"Well, it's actually for you."

"If you say so."

Joe helped Katie out of bed, and they got in the shower together. "You know, we don't always have to shower together," Katie said.

"I thought you liked showering with me."

"I do, but I don't look pretty anymore. My boobs are swollen, and my stomach is the size of a watermelon. I don't want you to see me looking like this."

Joe held Katie's arms and looked at her. "You are carrying another life inside of you. A life we created together. What could be more beautiful than that?"

They kissed. At first, it was a soft, tender kiss, but then it became passionate. After several seconds, Katie backed away and said, "I don't think so, Mister. I'm way too pregnant for that."

"That's funny because you weren't way too pregnant for that last night."

"Well, there has to be a tipping point sometime, and this is it. Besides, if you want us to see the sunrise, we need to hurry up and get ready."

"You are right as usual, my dear," Joe said.

When ready, they put on their coats and headed to the Three Eagles Ski Resort. The night shift was still on duty when they arrived. Katie waited at the front desk while Joe went to the garage and retrieved one of the snowmobiles the resort rents to guests. He drove it to the front door, where Katie met him. She put on the helmet and gloves that Joe had given her, and then they drove up the trail. Their destination was a spot near the summit with a beautiful view of the resort and the surrounding area.

Joe drove slower than usual. He didn't want to risk an accident in Katie's condition. When they neared the peak, Joe parked the snowmobile at the trail's edge, and they walked through a group of trees to a clearing. The locals called it "Lookout Point" because of the fantastic view. The sun had not yet risen, but the sky had a beautiful orange hue. The temperature was below freezing, but there was almost no breeze to make it feel colder.

"I'm glad you talked me into getting out of bed," Katie said. "It really is beautiful up here."

"That's why it's our favorite spot."

Katie put her head on Joe's shoulder and said, "My favorite spot is next to you."

Joe pulled her close. "I couldn't agree more."

They watched as the sky filled with bright orange and yellow hues. A bald eagle left its perch and swooped down the ski slope toward the resort. They stayed until a couple of minutes after sunrise.

"We should probably get back so you can do all those other things you have planned for me," Katie said.

As they started to walk away, Joe held Katie's arm and said, "Wait." He pointed toward the sun. "Do you see that?"

It had become a bit bright looking toward the early morning sun. Katie squinted and put a hand up to block the light. "It looks like a small plane. They fly over here all the time."

"I know, but don't you think this one is too low?"

Katie looked again. After watching it for a few seconds, she said, "You know, I think you're right."

They watched as the plane approached. It was smaller than most planes Joe had seen in his lifetime, and it was soon apparent that the aircraft was in trouble. "Pull up!" Joe yelled as if they could hear him.

"They're gonna crash," Katie screamed before the small plane disappeared into the trees about a hundred yards to their right. They heard a thunderous sound and then nothing. There was no flash of light and no explosion.

"Wait here," Joe said as he headed toward the snowmobile.

"No! I'm coming with you."

Joe stopped and put out his arm. "Fine, but we need to hurry."

They returned to the snowmobile as fast as Katie could walk. Joe opened the seat and took out a radio. There was no cell phone reception where they were. Michael, Joe's grandson and resort manager, kept a radio in his office. When he answered, Joe said, "Michael! A small plane crashed near Lookout Point. We're going to check it out. Call 911."

Joe quickly put the radio back where he got it and put the seat down. He then helped Katie onto the snowmobile and raced to where the plane went down. They found it upside down on the ground between two trees. Its wings had sheared off.

Joe ran to the aircraft and opened the nearest door. A woman hung upside down, still strapped in. Joe wasn't sure if she survived. He held her hand and connected to her. He could feel she was still alive, but she didn't have much time. She had a concussion, a couple of cracked ribs, and internal bleeding. The bleeding was a big concern, and he hesitated to let go, but he needed to check the pilot. He hoped the pilot wasn't as severely injured so he could come back and focus on the woman's injuries. He let go of her hand and moved to the other side of the plane. By then, Katie was there and asked, "Are they okay?"

"The woman is critical. I'm not sure about the man yet."

Joe opened the other door and held the man's hand. He tried to connect to him, but no life remained in him. "I'm afraid this one didn't make it," he told Katie.

Katie shook her head, "That's awful."

Joe quickly went back to the woman and held her hand. Katie stood next to him. "She's in serious condition. It will take me some time to stabilize her."

Joe unhooked the woman's seatbelt and gently carried her away from the airplane. He laid her on the ground and said to Katie, "See if you can find her coat." He then held the woman's hand and connected with her again. He concentrated on fixing the most severe issue first, the internal bleeding.

Katie went to the plane, opened the door, and looked inside. She saw the dead pilot hanging upside down and quickly looked away. She knew her comfort level wasn't as important as the woman's coat, so she looked inside again and saw two coats under the seats. She had to kneel, which was difficult for her, but she managed to pull both coats out of the airplane. She then stood and placed one coat over the woman's body and the other over her legs.

It took a while, but once the bleeding stopped, Joe worked on reducing the swelling in her brain. Ten minutes later, Eric, Michael's son, arrived on a snowmobile.

He walked up to Katie and asked, "Are they okay?"

"Joe is helping the woman now," Katie said. "I'm afraid the man didn't make it."

Eric shook his head. "That's a shame. The paramedics are here. Dad is setting them up with snowmobiles. I came ahead to see if I could help."

"I don't think so," Katie said. "Joe has it under control."

The woman suddenly opened her eyes, a look of confusion on her face. "What happened? Where am I?"

Katie knelt, held the woman's hand, and said, "You were in a plane crash. How do you feel?"

She looked around. "Steve! Steve! Where's Steve?"

Katie looked at Joe and then looked back at the woman. "I'm sorry. I'm afraid your companion didn't make it."

A look of shock came over the woman's face. "No! No, no, no, no. That can't be."

Tears streamed down the woman's face. "I can't believe it. He was so full of life."

"Was Steve your husband?" Katie asked.

"Husband? No. Steve is my boss. I mean, he was my boss," she said, wiping her tears.

"I'm so sorry," Katie said.

"His family will be devastated. And the company. I don't know how the company will survive."

She cried while Katie tried to comfort her. After a minute, she looked up and said, "My phone. I need to find my phone. I have to call my husband."

Katie shook her head and said, "You can't. Even if your phone survived the crash, there's no cell reception up here."

"What's your name?" Joe asked.

"Sonia. Sonia Wilson."

"Well, Sonia. I'm Joe, and this is my wife, Katie."

She wiped her tears again, looked at Katie, and said, "I thought you looked familiar. You're Katie Novak. I used to watch your human interest stories on the news."

"Thank you," Katie said. "I don't do that anymore."

"I know. You became an investigative reporter."

"That's right," Katie said. "It's nice to meet someone who watched the show. I wish it were under better circumstances."

Sonia wiped her tears again. "Yes. Me, too."

"I'm sorry again about your boss."

"Thank you. Are you certain he's gone? Maybe he's unconscious. I've heard it's easy to make that mistake."

"Joe has some medical experience. It's unlikely he's wrong."

Sonia closed her eyes for several seconds and took a deep breath. "I never lost anyone close to me before. I mean, I did lose one of my grandparents, my Dad's father, but I rarely saw him when I was growing up and hardly knew him."

"Losing people you love is something everyone experiences as they age," Joe said.

"Says the youngest person in the group," Sonia said.

Katie looked at Joe, smiled briefly, and then turned back to Sonia. "Joe is wise for his age."

"I'm curious. Why did you quit the news?" Sonia asked. "Was it because of the baby?"

"No. Joe and I got married, and I moved here to this beautiful place."

"That's too bad. I mean for the news station, not for you. How you and your husband solved all those crimes was impressive."

Katie looked at Joe. "Yeah, but that was in the past. Now we have a family to worry about," she said, looking down at her stomach.

"Yes. After all that, I would probably want to settle down, too. When are you due?"

"It won't be long now," Katie said. "Maybe another week. Maybe less. I don't have an official due date."

Sonia sighed. "I guess that's the circle of life. I'm very happy for you."

They heard the sound of snowmobiles and looked in that direction. After several seconds, one came around the corner, followed by two more. The drivers stopped on the trail and got off their vehicles. They all removed their helmets, revealing Michael and two paramedics. Michael walked over to Katie, Joe, and Eric while one of the paramedics checked on Sonia and the other checked on Steve North.

"Is everyone okay?" Michael asked.

"I'm afraid the pilot died in the crash," Joe said.

"Oh no," Michael said. He looked at Sonja and asked, "How is she?"

"She'll be okay. She still has a couple of cracked ribs that I didn't have time to fix."

Michael put his hand on Joe's shoulder and said, "She was fortunate you were up here when they crashed, Pops."

"That would make Katie the hero. If it weren't for her birthday, we wouldn't have come here to see the sunrise."

"That's right. Happy Birthday, Katie. I'm sorry. With all the excitement, I forgot. Well, I didn't forget completely. It just slipped my mind this morning."

"Thanks, Michael. It's okay. I haven't thought about my birthday since the crash."

When the paramedics finished treating Sonia, they removed the pilot from the plane and covered him. One of them approached the group and said, "We're almost ready to head back. Her injuries are surprisingly minor considering the crash killed the pilot."

Michael looked at Eric and asked, "Can you escort them back to the resort?"

"No problem," Eric said.

"Oh, and close the trail. We don't want tourists up here."

When the paramedics were ready, they put Sonia on the back of one of the snowmobiles and followed Eric back to the resort.

"I should get back, too," Michael said. "Are you two coming, or will you wait here for the coroner?"

"I should take Katie back so she can rest," Joe said. "I can bring the coroner back up here when he arrives."

"I'm staying with you," Katie said. "I don't need rest."

"Katie, you're almost nine months pregnant. You can't over-exert yourself like you used to."

"How am I over-exerting myself? I'm either standing still or sitting on the back of your snowmobile."

Joe was about to say something, but stopped. He thought momentarily and said, "You got me on that one."

"Listen, Joe. I appreciate your concern, but this is the first time in eight months that something exciting has happened around here. I don't want to miss it."

"Exciting things happen all the time around here," Joe said.

"Yes, but not like this."

"I get it," Joe said. "Once a newswoman, always a newswoman. You think exciting means newsworthy. I hate to say it, but there's no murder to investigate here."

"How do you know? Something caused that plane to crash."

"Most likely, it was a mechanical failure or pilot error."

"Pilot error? There were two people in that plane. Do you think neither of them saw the side of the mountain they were heading for?"

"I see your point, but mechanical failure still seems like the most likely cause."

"Whatever it was, I'd like to know."

"I wouldn't expect anything less from my curious wife," Joe said.

Michael interrupted, saying, "Maybe you two can continue your conversation inside the resort, where it's warm."

"Of course, Michael," Katie said. "Let's go back."

Chapter 3

When Katie and Joe returned to the resort, they found Detective Connor from the local sheriff's department waiting with two deputies.

"Detective Connor, it's good to see you again," Katie said. "I wish someone didn't have to die to prompt a visit." They had met her eight months earlier when someone murdered a man at Joe's resort.

"Unfortunately, it's the nature of the job, although my husband and I have talked about coming here for a day of skiing."

"That would be great," Joe said. "I'm sure you would enjoy it, and we'd like to meet your husband."

Conner looked at Katie and said, "My, you sure look different since I saw you last. When's the baby due?"

"Any day now. The sooner, the better."

"Well, I hope everything goes smoothly for you. We're just waiting for the coroner's people to pick up the body. Once they arrive, we'll need your help getting to the victim."

"Of course," Joe said. "We'll get the snowmobiles ready. Meet us out back by the garage when they arrive. Katie will show you the way."

Joe found Eric and asked for his help. They went to the garage and prepared six snowmobiles. Once ready, they brought them outside and attached a sled to the back of one of them.

Katie, Detective Connor, the two deputies, and two men from the coroner's office arrived a few minutes later. Joe, with Katie on the back of his snowmobile, led the group, followed by Connor and her deputies. The two men from the coroner's office followed the deputies. The man in the back pulled the sled that they planned to use to take the body off the mountain.

When they arrived at the wreckage, the two coroner's men prepared the body for transport. Connor looked at what was left of the airplane and said, "I can't believe someone survived this crash."

Katie glanced at Joe and then back at Connor. "She must have had a guardian angel."

They all slowly walked around the airplane when Joe noticed something. "Look at that," he said, pointing at the bottom of the aircraft just behind the wings, which was now at the top since the plane lay upside down.

"I don't see anything," Conner said.

"That's probably because I'm taller than you." He stepped close to the plane and turned to the closest deputy. "Can you give me a hand up?"

The deputy moved next to Joe, put his hands near Joe's feet, and locked his fingers together. Joe put a foot in his hands, and the deputy pulled Joe up high enough for him to get a good look. "Okay, you can let me down," Joe said after a few seconds.

The deputy let him down, and Connor asked, "What did you see?"

Joe put his fingers together in a circle. "There's a hole about the size of a cantaloupe. It was blown out from the inside."

The men from the coroner's office had put Steve North in a body bag and placed him on the sled. After they pulled the sled away from the aircraft, Joe looked inside one of the open doors and said, "Does anyone have a flashlight?"

Katie took out her phone, turned on the light, and handed it to Joe. He got on his back and slid under the seats. The airplane had only two seats. The area behind the seats was apparently for storage. He shone the light upwards and saw the hole from the inside. He then looked carefully at the surrounding area.

Joe slid back out, got to his feet, and returned Katie's phone to her. He shook his head, saying, "There's nothing back there except electrical wiring. Certainly nothing that would cause an explosion."

"That means someone planted an explosive device on the plane," Katie said. "Don't ever doubt my nose for news."

"Wait a minute," Connor said. "We can't assume sabotage until the NTSB gets here and examines the aircraft. That could take days or even weeks."

"When will they be here?" Joe asked.

"They should be here this afternoon. We're here to secure the crash site until they arrive."

One of the coroner's men approached and said, "We're ready to take the body now."

Joe led everyone back to the resort except the two deputies tasked with securing the crash site. They all met at the front desk, where Michael and Eric were helping guests. "I'm going to head out for a few hours," Connor said. "I'll return around lunchtime with a couple of deputies to relieve the two up there. I hate this babysitting duty."

"I bet the guys watching the plane don't care for it much either," Joe said.

"I was in their shoes once. I know how they feel."

After the detective left and no guests were around, Joe said to Eric, "Do me a favor. When you have some free time, take a thermos of hot coffee to the deputies at the crash site."

"Sure thing, Grandpa."

***

Twenty minutes later, Joe handled the front counter while Eric delivered the coffee to the deputies. Michael worked at his desk while Katie sat at the desk next to him and worked on marketing. The main door opened, and Sonia Wilson entered the lobby.

"Hello, Sonia," Joe said as she approached the front desk. "I didn't expect to see you here. How are you feeling?"

"Hi, Joe. I feel much better than I should. The hospital let me go. They said I have a couple of cracked ribs, so I need to take it easy until they heal, but nothing else is wrong with me."

"That's great news," Joe said. "You were fortunate."

"It's strange, though. I was unconscious until after you pulled me out of that plane, but the doctors found only a slight sign of a head injury. Nothing serious enough to cause unconsciousness or even a mild concussion. How is that possible?"

"That would be a question for your doctor."

"He suggested it might have been a psychological response to the crash, but I don't believe that."

"What do you think happened?" Joe asked.

"I have no idea. Maybe someone up there is looking out for me."

"That is certainly a possibility. So, what brings you here? Do you have no way to get home?"

"My husband is on the way to get me. I thought I would rather wait at your beautiful resort than at the hospital, so I took a cab here."

"Is that the only reason you are here?" Joe asked.

Sonia smiled. "You are quite perceptive for your age. The truth is, I wanted to talk to you and your wife."

"Really? What about?"

"Is Katie here? I'd like to talk to both of you."

Joe hesitated to get Katie because he had an idea what Sonia might want, but didn't want to be the kind of husband who hid things from his wife, even if it was for her own good. He said, "Just a minute," and walked into the office.

Katie was tapping away at her computer when Joe came in. "Honey, Sonia Wilson is here. She wants to talk to both of us."

Katie looked up, surprised. "Really? What does she want?"

"I can only guess."

Katie got up and joined Joe in the lobby. "Sonia, I didn't expect to see you here today. How are you feeling?"

"I'm a little sore, but I certainly don't feel like a plane crash survivor. I came here to thank you both for what you did for me today."

"We just happened to be in the right place at the right time," Katie said.

"I also wanted to ask for your help?"

"Our help? What can we do?" Katie asked.

"I don't think the crash was an accident. Everything was working fine, but suddenly, we heard a loud bang in the back of the aircraft. It was some kind of explosion. That's when Steve lost all control. I know that aircraft. I'm the vice president of sales. It's my job to know what I'm selling. Plus, my husband is the chief engineer. He helped design it. I can tell you there is nothing back there that would explode."

"We already figured that out," Katie said. "Joe climbed inside the plane and looked at the damage."

"That's exactly why I want your help," Sonia said. "Who else would have come to that conclusion so quickly?"

"What are you getting at? What do you need our help for?" Katie asked.

"I'd like you two to investigate this for me."

"I'm sorry, Sonia," Joe said. "We don't do that anymore. Besides, Katie is in no condition to start an investigation."

"Just a minute, Joe," Katie said. "I'd like to hear what she has to say."

"I can pay you," Sonia said. "I have money, and I'm sure I can get the company to pitch in. I'll pay you whatever the going rate is for private detectives."

"Wait," Katie said. "Let's start with why this is so important to you."

"Okay, I'll start at the beginning. Steve North had an idea for a battery-powered aircraft almost four years ago. He formed his company, Zero North, with the help of a few investors. He then hired my husband, Scott, who's an aeronautics engineer. Scott is actually employee number one. Steve wanted to create an affordable, practical airplane that ran on battery power. The 'Zero' represents the amount of carbon emissions released into the air."

"It looks like he succeeded," Joe said.

"He did, but I learned this morning that the company is almost out of money, and we have no more credit. That's why Steve was flying to Minneapolis. He planned to meet with a potential customer. He thought that if he could fly all the way from West Bend to Minneapolis, that would impress the customer. He also believed that securing a commitment from the customer to buy several planes would ease investor fears and enable us to get more funding. I talked him into letting me come along at the last minute."

"That doesn't explain why you need our help," Joe said.

"I know how these things go. The NTSB will eventually conclude that someone sabotaged the aircraft, but by then, the company might be bankrupt, and dozens of people could be out of a job, including my husband and me. We have a second prototype that is almost ready to fly. If you can prove that this crash was no accident, I believe we can fly that prototype to Minneapolis, and I can convince the customer to place an order. Then I can get the money we need from investors to keep the business afloat long enough to get the aircraft into production."

"Without your founder, won't that worry your investors?" Katie asked.

"I'm sure it will, but the groundwork has already been laid. Our prototype has proved itself in every way except range, and Steve was confident that wouldn't be a problem. Also, our Chief Operating Officer is a strong leader, and I believe he could easily step into the role."

"We would really love to help you, Sonia," Joe said, "but as I said, Katie is close to giving birth. We can't start an investigation now."

"Give us just a minute," Katie said. She took Joe's hand and led him to the supply closet. She closed the door and said, "Joey's not ready yet. I think we have time. We can do this. I'd really like to help her."

Joe shook his head. "I don't think that's a good idea. You don't want to do anything to complicate your pregnancy."

"I don't think asking a few questions will complicate anything, but I have you to uncomplicate it if it does."

"Did I ever mention that you are stubborn like a mule?"

"Maybe one or two dozen times."

Joe shook his head. "I hope I don't regret this."

Katie smiled and kissed Joe. "You're the best husband I've ever had," she said before stepping out of the closet.

Joe stepped out behind her and said, "I'm the only husband you ever had."

When they returned to Sonia at the front desk, Katie said, "Okay, we'll help you."

"But we can't make any promises," Joe added. "The health of Katie and the baby comes first."

"I completely understand," Sonia said.

"We're going to have lunch at the restaurant here," Joe said. "Would you like to join us? You can tell us about your company."

"That's a good idea," Sonia said. "I haven't eaten anything all day."

They walked to the restaurant and sat at a table near a window, which gave them a great view of the ski slopes. A few skiers were in sight, but the slopes were mostly empty, which wasn't unusual for a Tuesday afternoon.

Eric came to the table and said, "Good afternoon. My name is Eric. I'll be your server today."

"Katie looked at Joe and said, "You didn't?"

Joe laughed. "I did."

"I'll be right back, Katie," Eric said, smiling.

When Eric left, Sonia asked, "What was that all about?"

"You'll see in a minute," Katie said.

Eric returned, holding a cupcake with a burning candle.

"Oh, it's your birthday," Sonia said. "Happy birthday."

"Thank you, Sonia."

Several restaurant staff members joined Eric in singing Happy Birthday to Katie. When they finished, Katie blew out the candle and thanked everyone before they returned to their duties.

"How did you know that was going to happen?" Sonia asked.

"I met Joe a year ago yesterday, just before I turned thirty. On my birthday, he did the exact same thing to me."

"You're thirty-one years old? I don't believe it. I thought you were both in your early twenties."

Katie looked at Joe and back at Sonia. "Thanks. Joe is actually older than me."

"Oh, wow. I want to know your secret?"

"Good genes," Katie said, looking at Joe again.

Genetics was the most likely explanation for Joe's abilities and the abilities of generations of Healers before Joe. Still, Katie also entertained the idea that Joe might have descended from an angel mating with a human centuries ago.

Eric returned and took everyone's order. When he left, Joe said, "I have another surprise for you. This year, I had time to buy you a birthday present."

Joe reached into his pocket, took out a small gift, and handed it to Katie. Katie smiled, unwrapped it, and opened the box.

"Oh, my God!" she screamed as she removed a beautiful diamond bracelet. "I love it." She leaned over to kiss Joe and quickly put it on her wrist to admire it. "This is wonderful, but it's too much. You shouldn't have."

"It's okay. I know a guy at Ford Jewelers who got it for me at cost."

"Oh, that's right. In that case, well done, my dear."

"Are you talking about Mayor Ford?" Sonia asked.

"Yes. Former Mayor Ford." Katie said.

"I remember that story. I think that was when I became aware of how good you two are. I occasionally see an investigative reporter uncover a major crime, but it's rare. You solved three crimes in three months. Plus, that last one involved powerful political figures and police officers."

"Yeah, those were the days," Katie said.

Joe put his hand on Katie's stomach and said, "Our best days are yet to come."

Katie put her hand on Joe's, smiled, and said, "Of course. I can't wait."

"So, let's talk about your company," Joe said. "Can you think of anyone who would want to harm Steve North?"

"No. Absolutely not. Everyone loved Steve. He sometimes drove people hard, but he was right there with them. People appreciated that he wasn't afraid to get his hands dirty."

"What about people outside the company?" Katie asked. "Are there any competitors who are threatened by your company?"

Sonia thought momentarily and said, "Well, we have a competitor not far away in Milwaukee. The company is called 'Flight King Aviation.' A billionaire named Arthur King owns it. He made his fortune creating video games and wants to give back by making the skies less polluted. At least that's what he says on his website."

"You don't believe him?" Joe asked.

"I'm not one to judge, but Steve didn't care for him much, and he was a pretty good judge of character. Not perfect. I mean, he did hire some people who didn't work out for one reason or another, but I trusted his judgment."

"What did Steve say about Arthur King?" Joe asked.

"Steve said he had a big ego and only cared about how people saw him. He also said he thought King would set the world on fire simply for the glory of putting it out."

"Do you think he would resort to murder to eliminate his competition?" Katie asked.

"I don't know," Sonia said. "I do know we're not his only competition. We are the closest geographically, but other companies around the country are also developing electric airplanes."

"Are you ahead of Flight King?" Joe asked.

"Yes, a little. They started a little over two years ago, but have more staff and significantly more money backing them. As far as I know, they haven't produced a working prototype yet."

"That reminds me of the Wright Brothers," Joe said. "Their main competitors had deep pockets. A group of rich men, including Alexander Graham Bell, financed them. There's no proof, but rumor has it, Bell visited the Wright Brothers' workshop one day and peeked at some of their ideas while he was there."

"Did Orville tell you that?" Katie asked.

"Very funny. I do read, you know."

"That's an interesting story," Sonia said. "I don't think King would steal our ideas, but he did try to buy our company recently."

"Really? What happened with that?" Katie asked.

"Nothing. Steve turned him down. In hindsight, maybe he should have taken his offer. A little money would have been better than bankruptcy."

"You're not bankrupt yet, and you won't be if we can help it," Katie said.

Their food arrived, and they continued to discuss the company while they ate. When they finished, they returned to the front desk.

Chapter 4

Michael stood at the front desk, speaking to a tall, thin man with short brown hair and glasses. When they approached, the man saw Sonia and hugged her. "I'm so glad you're okay," he said. "That must have been very scary for you."

Sonia stepped back and said, "You took your sweet time getting here."

I'm sorry, Honey, but I was in the middle of testing our new rotors. I needed to finish what I started."

"Your wife was in a plane crash, and all you can think about is finishing your work," Sonia said, shaking her head.

Katie and Joe looked at each other.

"I'm sorry. You told me on the phone you were fine, so I didn't think you'd mind."

"Whether I'm fine or not isn't the point. Never mind. We'll talk about this later."

Sonia turned to Katie and Joe and said, "This is my husband, Scott. Scott, this is Katie and Joe. They pulled me out of the wreckage."

They shook hands, and Scott said, "I'm grateful to both of you."

"They are going to investigate and try to learn who did this," Sonia said.

"What do you mean, 'who did this?'" Scott asked. "Do you think it wasn't an accident?"

"There was an explosion where there shouldn't have been one. Joe confirmed it." She turned to Joe. "Can you take my husband up to see the damage?"

"Certainly," Joe said.

Scott looked at Sonia. "Wait a minute. How are these people qualified to investigate anything?"

"This is Katie Novak," Sonia said. "She used to be an investigative reporter for Channel 23 News."

Scott looked at Katie for a moment. "Oh, yeah. I thought I had seen you somewhere before. So, why would you investigate this if you're no longer a reporter?"

"Sonia asked for our help, and we thought we might be able to learn something for her," Katie said.

"Wouldn't that be a job for the police or the NTSB or whoever?"

"We can't afford to wait for them," Sonia said. "The company will be almost bankrupt before they learn anything."

"Bankrupt? What do you mean? How do you know that?"

"Steve told me this morning."

"Really? Why would he tell you and not me?"

"I'm sure that's not something Steve would want to worry his employees about," Sonia said. "He only told me because I pressed him."

Scott shook his head. "All this time, he acted so positively, like he didn't have a care in the world." He turned to Joe, "Okay, let's go look at the aircraft."

Joe led Scott to the garage and took out two snowmobiles. He closed the door and turned to Scott. "It's none of my business, but the key to a good relationship is always to put your wife's needs ahead of your own."

"You're right," Scott said as he got on the snowmobile. "It's none of your business."

"Do you know how to operate a snowmobile?" Joe asked.

"Of course," Scott said as he put on his helmet and started the engine. "I grew up in Wisconsin."

Joe led Scott up the trail to the wrecked airplane. The deputies guarding the plane differed from the two who came up with Joe earlier. "One of them said, "I'm sorry, but this is a restricted area."

"It's okay," Joe said. "I'm Joe Novak. I own this resort. This is Scott Wilson. He's an engineer for the company that built this airplane. He wants to take a quick look at the damage. We won't disturb anything."

The two deputies looked at each other, and the first one said, "I don't know."

"Call Detective Connor," Joe said. "She'll tell you it's okay."

The deputy took out his radio and stepped away. Two minutes later, he returned and said, "Okay, go ahead."

When they reached the plane, Scott said, "Do you really own this resort?"

"I do," Joe said.

"That's amazing. You're so young."

"Well, my grandmother gave it to me."

That was partially true. The woman he called his grandmother was actually his daughter, Susan. He gave the resort and all his investments to her after his first wife died over twenty years earlier. At that time, he changed his name and retreated into a reclusive life in his cabin. Gradually, he came out of his shell and started working at the resort when needed. It wasn't until he met Katie that he returned to a somewhat normal life. After Joe and Katie married and learned they had a child on the way, Susan felt it was time to return everything he had given her to him.

"You're a lucky guy," Scott said.

"In more ways than one," Joe replied.

Scott inspected the outside of the aircraft first. He opened one of the doors and shone a light from his phone inside the cabin. He got on his back and slid under the seats. After a couple of minutes, he slid back out, stood up, and said, "You were right. Someone planted a small explosive device in the aircraft. Whoever did this knew exactly what they were doing. This plane has no hydraulics. Everything is controlled by small electric motors. The person who did this placed the explosive at the junction of all that wiring. That meant Steve lost all steering and attitude control."

"You mean he was helpless up there?" Joe asked.

"He might have been able to control his speed, but without steering, that wouldn't have helped him much. Since they crashed long before their power would have been exhausted, I would guess the explosion affected the position of the flaps, which Steve couldn't compensate for. Fortunately, they came down fairly level. Steve was a great pilot. I bet he was able to bring the speed down as slowly as possible without stalling. He probably saved Sonia."

Joe nodded. "Yes. That was probably why she survived. So, if you are right, that means someone working on the project did this," Joe said.

"Maybe, but I can't think of anyone there who would have a beef with Steve or the company. The other possibility is that someone found our design on the internet. We engineers collaborate a lot online. Everything is password-protected, but hackers can be pretty smart. It might also have been a competitor who could have easily guessed how we wired our aircraft."

"That leaves open a lot of possibilities," Joe said.

Scott nodded. "I guess it does."

***

When Joe and Scott returned to the resort, they found Katie and Sonia seated in chairs near a window in the lobby. Across from them was a middle-aged woman, a young man in his early twenties, and a teenage girl, perhaps seventeen.

When they approached, everyone stood, and Katie said, "Joe, this is Helen North, Steve's wife, their son, Mark, and their daughter, Amy.

Joe shook their hands and said, "I'm very sorry for your loss."

"Thank you," Helen said.

Scott stepped in and hugged Helen. "I'm so very sorry, Helen."

"He died doing what he loved," she said, wiping tears from her eyes. "I would have never guessed when he left this morning that he would be flying his last flight."

"That shouldn't have been his last flight," Sonia said.

Helen looked at Scott. "Is it true? Did someone kill Steve?"

Scott slowly nodded. "It sure seems that way. The damage almost certainly couldn't have been accidental."

"Katie and Joe are going to help figure out who did this," Sonia said.

"We'll try to help, but we can't make promises," Joe said. "Katie's health takes priority."

Helen put her hand on Katie's arm. "If you can learn something, that would be great, but your baby should always be your top priority."

"Of course," Katie said, "but I think I will be okay for a while."

"I'm sorry, Mrs. North, but we need to ask you a couple of uncomfortable questions," Joe said.

"Please, call me Helen."

"Okay, Helen. Did you and your husband have a good relationship?"

"We had a great relationship. What does that have to do with what happened?

"Is there any chance at all that he might have cheated on you?"

Katie looked at Joe, surprised by the question. She knew Joe could sometimes be blunt when he questioned people, but occasionally, like now, he still caught her by surprise.

Helen's eyes narrowed, and a look of anger flashed across her face. "No! There is no way he would have cheated on me. Steve was not like that. I think this line of questioning is ridiculous. Why does my relationship with Steve have anything to do with his murder? You don't think I did it, do you?"

"I'm just trying to eliminate possibilities," Joe said. "A jaded lover or mistress could become very vindictive."

"Well, you can just scratch that possibility off your list. Steve was no cheater."

"I'm sorry I had to ask you that, but at least we eliminated that possibility," Joe said.

"Whoever did this wasn't a jaded lover. I don't know who would benefit from killing my husband, but I hope to God you find them and bring them to justice."

Joe nodded. "Will you be staying with us tonight?"

"Yes. Your father already checked us in. We need to wait for the autopsy before we can bring Steve home."

Michael, whom Helen called Joe's father, was actually Joe's grandson. When Joe last changed his identity, he became Michael's adoptive son. It had the potential to be awkward at times, but everyone knew their roles. Being ageless in the twenty-first century was difficult, but Joe knew someone who could change records for a price.

"We're heading back to West Bend. If you want to follow us, we can set you up in a hotel," Sonia said.

Joe looked at Katie and back at Sonia. It's Katie's birthday. I think we'll wait until the morning. I have a nice dinner planned for tonight."

Katie smiled. "Joe is a pretty adequate cook."

Joe looked at Katie and said, "If you think my cooking is only adequate, then I have definitely spoiled you too much."

"No, I think you've spoiled me just enough."

"Well, I hope you enjoy the rest of your birthday," Helen said. "We are going to get settled into our room."

"We're going to leave, too," Sonia said. "I'll text you the hotel information tonight."

Everyone said their goodbyes. After they left, Joe and Katie walked into the office where Michael was working at his desk. "We're going to take a few days off to investigate the plane crash," Joe said.

Michael looked up and said, "I'd expect no less from you two. Do you think you're up to it, Katie?"

"I think I can be equally uncomfortable no matter where I am."

"That's the spirit," Michael said. "We'll be fine here. I'm sure Mom will be glad to help out while you're gone."

"What about the NTSB?" Joe asked. "Can you help them, or should we wait until they arrive?"

"Don't worry about a thing, Pops. Go and enjoy the rest of Katie's birthday."

***

When Katie and Joe got home, Joe went into the kitchen and started preparing dinner. Katie stood in the doorway and asked, "What are you cooking tonight?"

"Only the best for my birthday girl. I bought a couple of nice filet mignons."

"Oh, nice. I feel so special."

"You are special, my dear. Now, sit on the sofa and relax. I'll take care of everything."

Katie sat on the sofa while Joe worked in the kitchen. She picked up a book she had been reading and settled in. Joe didn't have a television or a telephone when she met him. He didn't even have a radio or an indoor bathroom, for that matter. He lived a very simple life, relying on electricity for only his lighting and refrigerator. His heat came from a fireplace, and his stove used gas from a canister outside.

Their new home had a fireplace, but a furnace provided their primary heat. Katie admired Joe's rugged ways and didn't want to change him too much by bringing a television into the house. Even so, sometimes she wished she could sit back and watch a movie. For his part, Joe sometimes went to the movie theater with Katie, or they would attend a movie night at the resort.

Joe set the dining room table and poured two glasses of water. "It's almost ready, Honey," he said before returning to the kitchen.

A few minutes later, Joe returned to the dining room with a platter. He put a filet on each plate and added asparagus. He entered the living room and held his hand out for Katie. She held it as Joe helped her up from the sofa. "Uh," she said as she stood up. "I've had enough of this pregnancy thing."

"It won't be long now. Come. Enjoy your birthday dinner."

Katie sat down at the table and looked around. "Where's the steak sauce?"

"Are you kidding? Steak sauce is for bad steaks. You won't need it."

Katie cut her filet and took a bite. "Mmmm. You're right, Joe. This is delicious."

"Would I steer you wrong?" Joe said, stressing the word "steer."

"Don't quit your day job," Katie said before taking another bite of the steak.

After dinner, Joe washed the dishes and sat next to Katie on the sofa. "Can we feel the baby again?" Katie asked.

"Of course," Joe said, holding her hand and connecting with her. They became one person. Katie could feel everything Joe could feel, and Joe could feel everything, including the baby. Being able to feel all of your internal organs was an incredible feeling by itself, but also feeling your partner and your baby was beyond description. Katie assumed the baby could also feel what they felt, which greatly pleased her.

Chapter 5

The following morning, they packed a suitcase. They assumed they would only be in West Bend for a few nights, so they didn't need two suitcases. Joe did, however, bring a separate camera bag. He made a living as a photographer in his younger days, but that part of his life was over. Since then, photography has been his hobby. Occasionally, he would sell some of his photographs, but he didn't need the money. More often, he donated prints to charity auctions.

While Katie got ready, Joe put the suitcase and camera bag in the trunk. He returned to the house and brought out the child seat they bought for when the baby arrived. He didn't want to risk the baby being born without a proper car seat. When Katie was ready, they walked outside together, and Joe opened the passenger door for her. "Your chariot awaits, my dear," he said.

Katie walked to the driver's side, opened the door, and said, "It's my car. I'm driving."

Joe raced around to the other side, but was too late. Katie had already squeezed herself into the seat. Joe shook his head. "You are so stubborn."

"Yeah, I know. Just get in."

Joe got into the passenger seat and said, "Just drive slow. I'd hate for you to have a contraction while on the highway."

"I'll be fine. The baby's not ready yet. You know that."

"I don't know that for sure. I have no experience with babies."

"You had three kids, Joe."

"You know what I mean. I didn't know I could connect to other people back then."

"I'm not worried," Katie said. "I always feel safe when you're with me. I wish you could learn to worry less."

"I'm not worried. I like to be cautious. What's wrong with that?"

"You're only cautious because you worry too much," Katie said while she backed out of the driveway.

"Okay, so I worry. What's wrong with worrying? People get killed every day doing stupid stuff because they don't worry."

"What happened to Joe the optimist? You told me once that optimism is just a lack of worrying?"

Joe was silent for several seconds before saying, "I did say that, didn't I? Okay, you're right. I need to worry less, but ever since you almost died in that apartment explosion, I have felt overwhelmed with the responsibility of keeping you safe. I never want to feel what I felt that night again. When you became pregnant, that feeling of responsibility only grew."

Katie put her hand on Joe's. "I think that is why I feel safe when we are together, and I'm pleased you are protective of me. However, there's a difference between protective and overprotective."

"Yeah, I think it's David's fault."

"David? That was your middle child, right?"

"Yes. David was the daredevil of the family. He was always taking risks. I stopped him a few times when he was about to do something stupid, but I knew what it was like to be a young boy and didn't want him to remember his childhood as boring and restrictive."

"What happened?" Katie asked.

"He climbed a tree in our front yard when he was around six years old. I watched him go up. When he was about ten feet up, I said, 'Okay, David. That's high enough,' but he kept climbing. I should have been more forceful. I should have threatened to ground him if he didn't come down. I had been so lenient for so long that he didn't take me seriously."

"Oh, no! Did he fall?"

"A branch snapped, and he came down. He hit at least two large branches on the way down. I tried to catch him, but I wasn't fast enough." Tears formed in Joe's eyes. He wiped them with his hand.

Katie squeezed Joe's hand and said, "That's terrible. You must have felt awful."

"You can't imagine the guilt I felt. He ended up with a broken arm, multiple cuts and bruises, and a concussion. I wish I knew then what I know now about healing."

"Well, I guess I need to be more understanding the next time you nag me about my driving."

"Speaking of that, don't you think you're driving too fast?"

***

Sonia set them up in a hotel near the center of town in West Bend, but they arrived way too early for check-in, so they stopped at a small diner downtown for breakfast. They were met by a young woman who smiled and asked, "Two for breakfast?"

They both nodded and followed the woman to a booth. Katie put her hand on her stomach and said, "Uh, I don't do well with booths these days."

"Of course," the woman said, leading them to a table with chairs.

They both picked up their menus, and then Joe set his down. "You know, I don't feel comfortable having someone pay for our hotel."

"She hired us to do an investigation. That's normal."

"It's normal for private detectives, but that's not who we are. We're just average people."

Katie set her menu down and looked at Joe. "I hate to break it to you, Honey, but you are far from average."

"You know what I mean."

"I think I do. You're a nice guy who wants to help people for the pleasure of helping people. I get it. If you don't want to take money in exchange for helping Sonia, I am okay with that, but if you don't let her pay for our hotel, she will feel guilty, and I don't think you want to add guilt to all her troubles."

Joe was momentarily speechless. After a few seconds, he said, "Your logic is hard to argue with."

When they left the restaurant, Joe retrieved his camera from the car and took photos of the downtown area. He found many old, small towns to be visually appealing, and West Bend was no exception.

After leaving the downtown area, they drove to Zero North's headquarters. It was located in a large industrial park about a mile from the airport. There were several very long buildings, each with a garage door every forty feet or so and a regular door next to each garage door. Zero North occupied four units at the near end of the second building. The first door appeared to be the main entrance. The three doors to the right were not labeled.

Joe opened the first door and held it for Katie. He then followed her inside. There was a reception desk to the left, but nobody was there. To the right and a little further back were two more desks. A middle-aged man sat at the closest desk and looked up. He was about to say something when Sonia stood and said, "Katie. Joe. So glad you could make it."

"We're glad to be here," Katie said.

"Come in. Let me show you around." She put her hand on the shoulder of the man sitting at the desk and said, "This is Brian. He does our bookkeeping and also helps with customer service. We're a small company, and people wear different hats around here."

They shook hands, and Sonia led them to the office behind her desk. A man in his early forties sat behind a large oak desk. Sonia said, "Larry, this is Katie and Joe, the investigators I told you about." She turned to Katie and Joe. "This is Larry Cooper, our Chief Operating Officer."

Larry stood and shook Katie and Joe's hands. "I'm very pleased to meet you both. Sonia says you two are excellent investigators."

"We've had a few successes," Katie said.

"Well, I hope you can prove a design flaw didn't cause the plane crash. We need more money to finish what we started, and we won't get it if people believe our product is defective."

"Do you know why anybody would want to sabotage your aircraft?" Joe asked.

"I have no idea," Larry said. "I seriously doubt anyone who works here would want to hurt the company. Once we make our first sale, every employee will get a substantial bonus, and they know it. Who would want to ruin that?"

"What about Steven North?" Katie asked. "Maybe it wasn't the aircraft they were after. Maybe someone wanted him dead."

Larry leaned back in his chair and ran his hand through his hair. "Wow!" he said. "I hadn't considered that. Do you think this is about murder?"

"We don't know," Katie said. "What's more likely, murder or sabotage?"

Larry shook his head. "I would have never suspected either one was possible. I can't think of anyone who would want to kill Steve. Everyone loved him around here."

"What about outside the company?" Joe asked. "I hear you have a local rival that tried to buy your company."

"You mean Arthur King? I don't know him well, but I know his type—arrogant, self-important. He probably sees himself more as King Arthur than Arthur King, but he doesn't seem like the kind of guy who would kill to get what he wants. I doubt his ego would allow him to cheat. He needs to prove to the world that he's the best at whatever he does. I think he needs to prove it to himself, too."

"What if he's not the best?" Katie asked. "What if he's second best, and he knows it? Wouldn't his ego want to prevent the rest of the world from learning that fact?"

"Hmm. I hadn't thought of it that way. I guess that would be a question for a psychologist."

"How would you have felt if North sold the company to this King guy?" Joe asked.

"I don't know," Larry said. "I have a significant amount of money invested in this company. Selling would have kept me from losing my investment if we failed, but I would have also been out of a job. Additionally, I would have lost any chance of making a substantial amount of money if this company had succeeded.

"What about others in the company?" Joe asked. "Would they lose their jobs if King bought the business?"

"I'm sure some would go to the new company, but not all. I would guess if North did sell, he would have ensured that King compensated those employees somehow."

"Would any of your employees gain from the sale of the company?" Katie asked. "Other than not losing their jobs if the company failed."

Larry thought momentarily. "I don't see how, except some might have received a minor raise if they went to work for Flight King, which they would have gotten anyway if the company succeeded."

"We appreciate your time, Mr. Cooper," Katie said.

"Call me Larry. We're very casual around here." He picked up a business card and handed it to Katie. "If you have any other questions, please call me."

They said their goodbyes, and Sonia took them to the production room. On the way, Joe said, "I'm curious. Why does a company this size need a Chief Operating Officer?"

"Steve was an aircraft mechanic in the Air Force. He's always been a hands-on kind of guy. I think that's why the employees liked him. He spent a considerable amount of time working in the shop alongside the engineers and technicians. Larry came on board early because Steve needed someone to handle the business end."

"Was he here before you?" Joe asked.

"He started sometime after Scott and before me. Why?"

"I was just wondering how vested he was in the company."

"If you think Larry is the killer, you're wrong. You'll never convince me of that."

"We don't suspect anyone at the moment," Joe said.

Inside the production room were three aircraft in various stages of construction. One looked complete, except its wings were lying on the floor next to it. About a dozen employees worked on numerous projects inside the room. To their right was a small break room, about the size of a typical bedroom, with large glass windows overlooking the production floor. An identical room was to their left, with three people inside looking at a blueprint placed on a table in the center of the room.

Sonia opened the door to the left and led them inside. Everyone inside stopped what they were doing and looked at their new visitors. Sonia's husband, Scott, stood to the right of the table. Behind him were three computer workstations set up so the users could see what was happening in the production room.

A tall, somewhat portly man with short brown hair and a beard stood to the left. Behind him stood a copy machine and a large printer, probably used for printing the blueprint they were looking at.

Between them was an attractive young woman. Her long, blond hair was tied behind her head. She looked up and smiled. "Hi, Sonia," she said in a slight Russian accent.

"Hi, Elena. This is Katie and Joe Novak. They are here to investigate the plane crash." She pointed to her husband and said, "You already know Scott." She then pointed to Elena. "This is Elena Petrova, and the big bear next to her is Max Allen."

Max laughed and held out his hand. They all exchanged greetings, and Sonia said, "I have some work I need to finish. Please answer any questions they might have and, if you don't mind, Scott, can you show them around the shop afterward?"

"Sure thing, Honey."

When Sonia left, Joe said, "You have an impressive operation here." He pointed at the airplane, which looked almost complete, and said, "Is that airplane there ready to fly?"

Scott turned to look and said, "It's close." The crash taught us we have a significant vulnerability. We are working to add wireless controls to the steering mechanisms as a backup. It will add a little cost and weight to the final product, but it'll be worth it."

"Are any of you pilots?" Katie asked.

"I am," Elena said. "I learned from my father. He was a fighter pilot in the Russian Air Force."

"That's interesting," Katie said. "Does he live here now?"

"Yes, he does. He had to leave the service when I was young because he developed back problems."

"Oh, that's too bad," Katie said. "I didn't know back problems would keep someone from flying."

"It will if you're a fighter pilot. The high G-forces can put a lot of stress on the body."

"That makes sense," Katie said. "How did you end up in the United States?

"My dad's cousin owned a furniture store here in West Bend and wanted to expand. He offered my dad a stake in the company for a small investment and his help in running the business. So, when I was eight years old, I moved to America with my parents and older brother."

"That must have been hard for you," Katie said.

"It was at first. I knew very little English. Now, I'm glad we moved here. I feel proud to be an American."

"So, will you be test-flying the aircraft you're making here?" Joe asked.

"I hadn't thought about that. Maybe. Larry is also a pilot. He might become our new test pilot. Or maybe Scott could do it once he gets his license."

Katie looked surprised. "Oh, you're learning to fly, Scott?"

"Yeah. I thought it would be fun. Steve was teaching me. He's a certified instructor. I mean, he was a certified instructor."

"What about you, Max?" Joe asked.

"Me? I prefer to keep my feet on solid ground."

Joe pointed out the window and asked, "Can we go out there?"

"Sure," Scott said. "Unfortunately, I'm in the middle of something important." He looked at Max. "Can you show them around, Max?"

"No problem," Max said. He opened the door for Katie and Joe, who followed him into the production room.

"Is there anything in particular you want to see?" Max asked.

Joe pointed at the nearly complete aircraft. "Can we see that one?"

"Of course," Max said, leading them out the door and past the two partially completed aircraft.

Joe walked halfway around the plane and returned to Katie and Max. "Is this exactly the same as the one Steven North flew?"

"Mostly," Max said. "We made some minor improvements to the software, and we're working on adding wireless controls so what happened to Steve won't happen to anyone else."

"Software?" Joe asked.

"Yes. This plane is capable of flying on its own. A person just needs to enter the destination, set it to auto, and it will fly there. The pilot is only needed for takeoffs, landings, or any emergencies that might arise."

"So it's like autopilot?" Katie asked.

"Yes and no. I guess you can call it super autopilot. We hope to have a fully automated aircraft that will take off and land without human assistance within the next five years."

"That's impressive," Katie said. "What will the pilot be needed for then?"

"Not much," Max said. Many crashes are caused by human error. We hope to eliminate that."

"It used to be new technology took over menial jobs, like assembly lines," Joe said. "Now, everyone with a skill has to worry about losing their jobs."

"That's progress, I guess," Max said.

"What will you do when artificial intelligence takes over your job?" Katie asked.

"Hopefully, that won't happen anytime soon. I suppose if it did, I would be forced to get one of those menial jobs you mentioned."

"How ironic that humans are working hard to change places with machines," Joe said. "I said it before: technology is not our friend."

"Maybe not, but it's here to stay," Max said.

"Let's talk about the autopilot," Katie said. "Was it running when the plane crashed?"

"We would have to wait for a report from the NTSB to know for sure, but I doubt it. Steve liked to be in control of the aircraft. Even if it were active, any attempt to control the plane manually would automatically disengage it."

"Can we look inside?" Joe asked.

"Sure," Max said and opened the passenger side door.

The plane had a short one-foot stub of a wing that was covered with anti-slip tape. It was obviously meant to be a step. Under the step was a hole into which the main wing would slide. Joe stepped up and stuck his head inside. He knelt on the seat and looked behind it. There was an empty space big enough to hold a couple of suitcases. Behind that was an access panel held on with four screws. It blocked access to the rear of the plane.

Joe sat on the seat and stuck his head out the door. "There's a panel behind the seats that wasn't on the other one."

"Oh, yes," Max said. "That's the other change we made. It makes it a little harder for anything dangerous to get back there."

Joe closed the door and pushed the button to lock it. He then unlocked it and exited the plane. Katie asked, "What do you think?"

"I think without that panel, someone could have easily tossed a small explosive device behind the seats and have it land exactly where they needed it to land."

"Did Steve keep his plane locked?" Joe asked.

"Steve's plane didn't have locks on the doors. We added those to the newer version."

"That's another thing you forgot to mention," Joe said.

"I'm sorry. Those were incorporated into this aircraft long before the accident. I didn't think about it."

"Tell me, Max," Katie said. "Do you like your job here?"

"Sure. It's very rewarding."

"Did you get along well with Steve North?"

"Oh, yes. He was a good man."

"What about your coworkers?" she asked. "Do you all get along, or is there conflict?"

"Well, uh, you know. Everybody's different. It's probably impossible to get along with everyone, but it's nothing I can't handle."

"Who don't you get along with?" Katie asked.

"It's not that I don't get along with them."

"Them?" Joe asked.

Max looked behind him briefly and whispered, "Scott and Elena."

"Scott and Elena?" Katie whispered back. "What's wrong with them?"

"Why are we whispering?" Joe asked. "They can't hear us."

"What's wrong with Scott and Elena?" Katie asked again, a little louder.

"Well, there's nothing wrong with them. It's just that they spend their time flirting with each other. I feel a little like a third wheel in there."

"Katie's eyes widened. "Really? Is Scott having an affair with her?"

"I don't know," Max said. "I try to mind my own business."

"Does Sonia know?" Katie asked.

"I doubt it, and I'm not going to tell her. Maybe it's just innocent flirting. Why ruin a marriage for that? Besides, things have cooled between them since the accident."

"I think we've taken up enough of your time, Max," Joe said. "Thank you so much. We can find our way out."

As Katie and Joe walked back toward the office, Katie asked, "What's wrong? Why did we leave so quickly?"

"Because I know you. We're not here to investigate someone's marriage."

"I know, but don't you think Sonia deserves to know the truth?"

Joe stopped walking and turned to look at Katie. "What truth? That her husband is flirting with someone? Do you want to wreck a marriage over that?"

"We wouldn't be the ones wrecking the marriage."

"Listen. I am definitely not a fan of Sonia's husband, but we need to remember we are here investigating a murder. Sonia's personal affairs are Sonia's personal affairs."

"I know, but..."

"Please, Katie. Promise me you won't say anything."

After a brief pause, Katie said, "Fine. I won't say anything."

They returned to the office and found Sonia on the phone. She held up a finger and quickly finished her conversation. Upon hanging up, she asked, "Did you guys learn anything useful?"

"We learned plenty," Katie said before Joe nudged her side. "We're just not sure any of it is relevant to the case."

"So, is there anything else I can help you with?" Sonia asked.

"Yes," Joe said. "You can show us the hangar where you stored the plane."

"Certainly. Would you like to ride with me, or do you want to follow me?"

Katie looked at Joe, who shrugged. "We'll follow you," she said. "We should be able to check into our hotel afterward."

Chapter 6

They followed Sonia to the airport. It was a small airport and not very busy. They parked behind the hangar and followed Sonia to the back door on its left side. She punched a code on the keypad and opened the door. Once inside, she deactivated the alarm.

The hangar was relatively small, barely large enough to accommodate two small aircraft. It was nearly spotless and free of the smells associated with aircraft maintenance. To the right of the door was a small table with a coffee maker. Beyond that was a sofa with a small coffee table in front of it. In the far right corner was a small enclosed office. There were no aircraft inside, but several pieces of equipment were scattered around the perimeter, including a large tool cabinet, a workbench, and several shelving units filled with aircraft parts.

"How do you get the planes from the factory to here?" Katie asked.

"The wings are designed to come off easily. With the wings off, two will fit inside a semi-trailer," Sonia said.

"I hope the wings are designed to stay on easily, too," Joe said.

Sonia laughed, "I assume you're kidding."

Joe didn't reply.

"Are there cameras in here?" Katie asked.

"I wish there were," Sonia said. "Steve didn't want his employees to feel like he was spying on them. I guess he never imagined someone would do something so terrible."

"Is there another way in?" Joe asked. "Can someone open the main door from the outside?"

"Yes. There's a keypad for that door, too."

"Is it the same code?" Joe asked.

"Yes. There's also a physical key, but I think only Steve had that."

"Who knows the code?" Katie asked.

"Well, let's see. Besides Steve, there is me, Larry, Scott, Max, and Elena."

"What about the alarm code?" Joe asked. "Is it different than the door code?"

"Yes, it is. Of course, everyone who knows the door code also knows the alarm code."

"Is there only one alarm code, or do you each have your own code?" Katie asked.

"No. There's only one code."

"Is there a record every time someone enters the code?" Joe asked.

"I suppose there is, but we wouldn't have that. I'd have to talk to someone at the alarm company."

"Please do that," Joe said.

They left the hangar and walked back to the parking lot. Sonia said, "I know you want to get settled into your hotel, but I'd like to invite you for dinner tonight.

Katie looked at Joe, who nodded. "We'd like that," she said.

"Good. I'll text you my address. How does seven o'clock sound?"

"That's perfect," Katie said.

***

After leaving the hangar, Katie and Joe headed to their hotel. It was a newer-looking three-story building near the center of town, about a block from the Milwaukee River. As they checked in, Joe requested a room on the first floor. The woman behind the counter looked at Katie and said, "I understand. Room 106 is available."

Their room was small but clean. The bathroom was to the left, near the door, and the closet was to the right. The room had a king-sized bed, a couple of chairs, a small refrigerator, and a coffee maker. Katie opened the curtains, which revealed a large brick building belonging to a construction company across the street. The sign on the building read, "Torres Kirk Homes."

"Here we are, living in hotels again," Katie said.

"Are you unhappy about that?" Joe asked.

"No, not at all. I mean, I do like sleeping in our own bed, but I love this investigating business."

"Yes, I know you do. Just remember, when the baby is born, we will have more important things to think about."

"I realize that Joe and I look forward to being a mother, but right now, I want to do something good for someone else, even if it's the last time."

"I have a feeling it won't be the last time. I can picture you solving murders while little Joey is in preschool."

Katie smiled. "Not me. We will be solving murders."

"We. Of course." Joe put his arms around Katie and kissed her.

The kissing became passionate until Katie pulled away and said, "That's enough. I think you can wait until after the baby comes."

Katie sat on the bed, and Joe sat next to her. He put his arm around her and said, "Whatever you wish, My Dear."

Katie put her hand on Joe's knee and looked at him. "It's not what I wish, Joe. I want to have sex, too, but look at me. Everything is so uncomfortable right now."

"I know. I wish I could help you, but it's a natural part of being pregnant."

"Oh!" Katie said suddenly, putting her hand on her stomach.

"What is it? Are you okay?"

Katie took Joe's hand and placed it on her stomach. "The baby's kicking. Do you feel it?"

"I do," Joe said, smiling.

"Can we connect to the baby again? I'm sure he can feel us, too, and I think it comforts him to know we are both here for him."

"Of course," Joe said, helping Katie sit back against her pillows. He sat next to her and held her hand. He concentrated, and soon, they were connected as one person. They could both feel everything, including the baby.

"I wish I could tell what he is thinking," Katie said.

"He's thinking how lucky he is to have such a wonderful mommy."

Katie laughed. "He's not thinking that."

"He may not be thinking it, but he is feeling it?"

Katie squeezed Joe's hand. "I just want him to be happy."

"As do I, and I think he's off to a great start."

***

They left the hotel a couple of hours later as snow started falling. When they reached Katie's car, Joe asked, "Are you sure you don't want me to drive? I know driving in the snow is not your favorite thing to do."

"I will never live that down, will I?"

"You mean driving into me with your car during a snowstorm? No. I will be sure to remind you from time to time."

"Thanks a lot, Joe, but I'm fine. If I hit anyone else, I'll have you fix them up."

"Let's try not to hit anyone."

"Okay," Katie said. "If you insist."

They drove to the address that Sonia had given them. The neighborhood looked relatively new. Joe figured it was five years old, eight tops. He made his deduction not by looking at the houses but at the trees. There were no mature trees in the entire neighborhood. He thought it was a shame that some developers plow down every tree in their developments before building. He had seen some new developments that were environmentally friendly, but that was the exception.

They pulled into the driveway of a beautiful, two-story farmhouse-style home with a two-car garage. Joe helped Katie out of the car, and they walked to the front door. Before they could ring the bell, the door opened. A smiling Sonia said, "Katie. Joe. Welcome. Come on in."

They followed Sonia to the living room, where Scott watched television on the sofa. A large ginger cat slept on the cushion next to him. When Scott saw them, he turned the television off and stood to greet them.

"You have a nice home," Joe said.

"It was a wedding gift from my parents," Sonia said.

"Wow! That's amazing," Katie said. "Are your parents rich?"

"They do very well. My parents moved here from Puerto Rico when my mom was pregnant with me. My dad was a carpenter and worked for a large builder with developments all over the eastern half of the United States. They had a project in Milwaukee that desperately needed skilled carpenters. It was a chance to earn good money, so he and Mom packed their belongings and moved here. When I was around six, my dad partnered with a coworker, and they started their own construction company right here in West Bend. They built this entire neighborhood and a few others."

"I don't suppose their company is called Torres Kirk Homes?" Joe asked.

"It is. How did you know?"

"Lucky guess," Joe said.

Sonia looked at Joe briefly, and then a smile slowly came to her face. "Lucky guess, my ass. You saw it from your hotel."

Joe laughed. "You caught me. I'd like to say that I'm a psychic, but I have no such skills."

Katie glanced briefly at Joe. "He's not a mind reader, anyway."

"Dinner will be ready soon," Sonia said. "Let's have a seat at the table."

Sonia led them to a large dining room. To the right, a fire burned in a fireplace. To the left, four large windows overlooked the front yard. It was dark outside, but the streetlights illuminated a light snowfall. The table was large enough to sit eight, and a beautiful chandelier hung above it. Katie and Joe sat with their backs to the windows, and Scott sat across from them.

Sonia went into the kitchen and came out with a bottle of wine. She removed a fancy electric corkscrew from a box and asked, "I know you can't have any, Katie, but would anyone else like a glass of wine?"

Katie kicked Joe in the shin and subtly motioned for him to say something.

Remembering Sonia was pregnant, Joe said, "Oh, uh, do you think we can all skip the wine today? I have been sober almost two years now and don't want to be tempted."

"Of course, Joe," Sonia said, putting the corkscrew back in the box. "That is quite an accomplishment. I wouldn't want to do anything to set you back."

Sonia returned the wine to the kitchen, and Katie asked, "Is there anything I can do to help?"

"Don't be silly, Katie. You relax. I have everything under control."

Sonia returned with a large salad bowl and put salad on everyone's plate. She then sat next to her husband. "How is your hotel room?" she asked. "Is it comfortable?"

"Nothing is truly comfortable right now," Katie said, "but it's fine."

"I can't imagine what you're going through," Sonia said. "Scott and I talked about having children, but we're not ready yet."

"I think you would be surprised by what you are ready for," Joe said.

"Yes," Katie said. "The idea that I will soon bring another life into this world is such an incredible feeling. At first, I wasn't sure if I was ready to be a mother, but now I can't wait. I'm sure when the time comes, you will feel the same way."

"I hope so, and I'm very happy for you both," Sonia said.

When everyone finished their salads, Sonia collected their plates and brought lasagna to the table. She put some on everyone's plate and then gave them each a slice of garlic bread.

Katie took a bite and said, "This is delicious." She turned to Joe. "I think you have some competition for chef of the year."

"Oh, you like to cook, Joe?" Sonia asked.

"I find cooking to be quite relaxing."

"I know what you mean," Sonia said.

"What about you, Scott?" Katie asked. "What do you do to relax?"

"The only thing I find relaxing is relaxing. Sometimes, I work ten to twelve-hour days. When I get home, I just want to veg out on the sofa. Cooking is too much like work, and work is the opposite of relaxing as far as I'm concerned."

"I can understand that," Joe said. "Those are long days. Do you ever go out with your coworkers after work?"

"Not too often. Occasionally, a few of the guys and I will go out after work for a beer or two if we get off early enough."

"Just guys?" Katie asked before Joe nudged her side. "I mean, a lot of women like to go out for a drink too."

Scott hesitated and said, "The women do their own thing."

"Does anyone want more bread?" Sonia asked.

Katie and Joe both shook their heads. "No, thank you," Katie said.

"Speaking of going out," Katie said, "how are the social dynamics at the company? I mean, does everyone get along? Are there social cliques, or is it like a big, happy family?"

Scott looked at Sonia, who said, "I think it is like a big happy family at work, but there are some cliques that hang out after work. There's no animosity between anyone if that's what you're getting at."

"What about former employees? Joe asked.

"Nobody has left the company in six months or so," Sonia said.

"Why did the last person leave?" Joe asked.

"That would have been Alan Hutchinson. He was an engineer." Sonia looked at Scott. "You worked with him. Why did he leave?"

"He was always complaining about his pay. He wanted to make more money than I was making. Steve told all of us that we would get a big raise once the company became profitable, but Alan couldn't wait. He left to take a job with Flight King Aviation."

"That's when Steve hired Elena," Sonia added.

"Did Alan know the code to get into the hangar?" Joe asked.

"Yes, he did, but I think Steve changed it after he left," Scott said.

Sonia nodded. "It's common to change the codes when employees leave."

"Was the alarm code also changed?" Joe asked.

"I believe it was," Sonia said.

"Would there be any reason this Alan guy might want to sabotage the company?" Katie asked.

"No. Not on his own," Scott said, "although I wouldn't put it past him to do something like that for money."

"Really?" Sonia asked. "I didn't know him as well as you, but he didn't seem like the type of person who would kill someone for money."

"I don't know," Scott said. "He mostly kept to himself about his personal life. Who knows what he was hiding? I only know he was all about making more money. Maybe he was in debt or something."

"That's interesting," Katie said. "Do you think this King guy might have paid him to sabotage the airplane?"

"I don't know. Maybe. Anything's possible."

"I think we need a lot more evidence before we assume anyone is guilty," Joe said.

"I totally agree," Sonia said. "This is all speculation now. Besides, Alan doesn't know the new codes."

"I'm sure a billionaire like King could hire someone to break in unnoticed," Scott said. "The hangar is not exactly Fort Knox. Maybe Alan didn't do it, but instructed the guy who did."

"I think we need to go to this Flight King Aviation tomorrow," Katie said.

After dinner, Joe helped Sonia clean up while Katie sat at the table and talked to Scott. She didn't quite know what to say to him. "So, what do you and Sonia do in your free time?"

"Not much. We don't have a lot of free time."

Joe helped Sonia wash dishes. He washed them while she dried them and put them away. "This is a big house for two people," Joe said. "Did you have any say in its construction?"

"Yes and no. This was one of the model homes for this neighborhood. After the neighborhood was completely sold, the model homes were then sold. Before that happened, my parents gave me a choice of which home I wanted. I liked this one because it was the only four-bedroom house."

"Did your parents give the house to you only or to both of you?"

"Technically, it's in my name, but since we are married, it belongs to both of us."

"A four-bedroom house is bigger than average. Did you plan on having more than two children?"

"I didn't really have a plan. I thought it was possible. I wanted to be prepared just in case we did, but you know what they say, 'Man plans and God laughs.'"

"You're still young. I think you would make a great mom."

"Thanks, Joe. We'll see."

***

As they drove back to their hotel, Joe asked, "So, what do you think about that Alan guy? Do you think Arthur King would trust him to do something highly illegal after knowing him for only six months?"

"I don't know. What is the minimum amount of time you should know someone before asking them to commit murder for you?"

Joe shook his head. "I don't know. I wouldn't kill for someone I've known for a hundred years."

Katie glanced at him. "Who have you known for a hundred years?"

"Well... no one who's still alive, but even if my best childhood friend were alive and in trouble, I wouldn't kill for him."

"You killed someone for me," she reminded him.

"I did it to save your life. You know that."

"I know, and I love you for that. I also know it wasn't easy for you."

"At the time, it was an easy choice. He tried to kill you. If I hadn't stopped him, he would have succeeded, but I didn't murder him. He forced me to choose between your life and his. I would never murder someone."

"Unfortunately, Joe, everyone is not like you. Some people don't care about human life. It is those people who are hardest to understand. For someone like that, six months might be plenty of time."

"Or two someones," Joe added.

"That's right. Maybe Alan Hutchinson and Arthur King are both psychopaths."

"Psychopaths are good at appearing normal. It may be hard for us to know," Joe said.

"Well, we'll just have to confirm everything they tell us."

When they arrived at their hotel, they followed a woman through the main door. She was in her mid-thirties and had long, blonde hair. She wore a black pantsuit and a long, gray wool coat. Once inside, the woman stopped walking and started coughing. It was a deep, persistent cough that continued for more than ten seconds.

Joe stepped in front of her and asked, "Are you okay? Do you need help?"

The woman held up a hand. "Don't come any closer. I seem to have picked up something nasty." She sniffled. "It's awful timing because I have an important presentation tomorrow."

"It's okay," Joe said, stepping in closer. "I'm immune."

She raised an eyebrow. "How could you know that? You don't even know what I have."

"My husband has quite the immune system," Katie said.

Joe extended his hand. "Give me your hand. I can help you."

"How can you help me?"

"Just give me your hand, and I'll show you."

Reluctantly, the woman held out her hand, and Joe took it in his. He connected to her and soon felt the virus that had invaded her body. He didn't know what kind of virus it was, but it didn't matter to him. A virus was a virus. "You have a virus," he said.

She frowned. "How could you know that by holding my hand?"

Joe ignored the question and continued, "When a virus enters the body, the immune system gets to work. It first identifies the invader and then produces antibodies to fight it. If your immune system is weak, this process is slow." He started massaging the palm of her hand. "There are pressure points in our hands that, if stimulated just right, can speed up antibody production."

As far as Joe knew, there were no such pressure points, but he needed the time to direct the woman's immune system to increase the necessary antibodies to fight the virus. After a few minutes, he said,

"Now, you need to do one thing: rest. Rest is a time of healing. Try to get as much sleep as possible tonight, and you will feel fine tomorrow."

She looked skeptical but was polite. "It seems hard to believe, but I hope you're right."

She thanked Joe and headed to the front counter while he and Katie went to their room. When they entered, Katie kissed Joe. "That was a nice thing you did. I'm so lucky to have such a thoughtful husband."

"I'm the lucky one," Joe said, kissing her back.

"Yes, you are. I hope you never forget that."

"I'm sure you will remind me."

Katie kicked off her shoes, took Joe's hand, and led him to the bed. "You can count on that," She said before sitting on the bed and pulling him down next to her.

"You want to make love? I thought you said you're too pregnant for that."

"I don't want to make love. Well, I do, but that's not what I want right now. I want to feel how the baby is doing."

"I'm sure the baby is no different than he was when we felt him three hours ago."

"Well, if you don't want to," Katie said, looking away.

Joe sighed. "You are quite the manipulator. Okay, fine."

Katie looked back at Joe and smiled. "I knew you'd see it my way."

They both got comfortable on the bed, and Joe connected to Katie. Soon, they could both feel the baby. After several minutes, Katie said, "I think he's ready."

"I think he's ready, too, Katie, but it is ultimately your body's decision. Unfortunately, this is all new to me. I don't know what normal is."

"Can't you induce labor? I don't know if I can last another week."

"I've never done anything like that before, and I certainly don't want to experiment on you. Besides, don't you want to find out who killed Steven North?"

Katie was silent for a moment, then sighed. "Well, since you put it that way, I suppose little Joey can wait a few more days."

Chapter 7

The following morning, while eating breakfast in the hotel restaurant, the woman Joe helped in the lobby approached them. She put her hand on Joe's arm and said, "Good morning. Whatever you did to me yesterday worked wonders. I feel great this morning. Thank you so much."

"It was my pleasure to help," Joe said.

"I never heard of pressure points being used to treat viruses. Where did you learn that?"

"I come from a long line of natural healers," Joe said.

"I should probably introduce myself. My name is Cynthia Taylor. I'm from a nonprofit organization called the Foreign Wars Preservation Society. We have a collection of never-before-seen World War II photographs at the Art Museum in Milwaukee for the next two weeks." She reached into her purse and pulled out several tickets. She handed two tickets to Katie and Joe. "I'd love to see you there. I hope you can come."

Katie looked at Joe and asked, "Didn't you donate all your Great-grandfather's World War II photos?"

"Yes. That was several months ago. I can't remember who I gave them to, though."

"Your great-grandfather had photos from the war? What was his name?" Cynthia asked.

"Joe Young. He was a combat photographer in North Africa."

"You're kidding? That's quite a coincidence. Almost half of our collection is photographs taken by Joe Young. Now you must come. I won't take no for an answer."

Joe looked at Katie, who shook her head, "No, thank you. I've seen some of his photos. They are too disturbing for me."

"Yes, they are," Cynthia said. "That is why people need to see them."

Katie looked puzzled. "What do you mean? Why should people look at disturbing photos?"

"Because no one should ever think of war as a game to be won or lost. It is a tragedy for both sides. If people would remember that, maybe wars could become a thing of the past."

After a brief pause, Katie said, "I guess that makes sense. I suppose I should know what my husband went through. I mean my husband's great-grandfather."

"That's great," Cynthia said. "I will be there all day today. I hope to see you there."

***

After breakfast, Joe and Katie headed to Milwaukee. They drove for thirty minutes and found Flight King Aviation a few blocks north of a small airport in the city's northwest area. The airport resembled the one in West Bend: too small for commercial airliners but ideal for small, experimental aircraft.

Flight King Aviation was in an industrial park, similar to Zero North's headquarters. Unlike Zero North, they occupied an entire building that was more than double the size of Zero North's operation. Katie parked the car, and they went inside.

They entered a large, modern-looking room. They could hear the sound of machinery in the background. To their right was a waiting area with four chairs, two on one wall and two on another. Several pictures hung on the walls. Some were drawings of a small aircraft. Others were photos of airplanes in various stages of completion. To the left was a counter. Beyond the counter, a woman sat behind a desk.

When the woman saw Katie and Joe, she stood from her desk and walked to the counter. "Good morning. How can I help you?"

Katie approached the counter and said, "Hi, I'm Katie Novak, and this is my husband, Joe. We want to speak with Mr. King. I'm sure he's busy, but this will only take a few minutes."

"Can I ask what this is about?" she asked.

"We are private investigators looking into the death of Steven North."

"Oh, I heard about that. It was quite tragic, but I don't see how Arthur can help you."

"Maybe he can't," Katie said, "but we'd like to find out."

"Just a minute," the woman said before stepping through a door to her left. She returned a minute later and said, "Follow me, please."

She led them down a short hallway and opened the second door on the left. "Go right in," she said.

They were in a relatively small office, considering Arthur King was a billionaire. It looked more like the office of a middle manager. King was sitting behind his desk to their right. He looked young for a man of forty. He was clean-shaven with short, dark hair and brown eyes. He dressed casually, wearing a blue polo shirt with the company logo: a smiling airplane wearing a crown. He stood up and held out his hand. "Hi. I'm Arthur King."

They shook hands, and Katie and Joe introduced themselves.

"Have a seat," King said, motioning to the two chairs in front of his desk.

Katie and Joe sat down, and Katie said, "Thank you for seeing us, Mr. King."

"Call me Arthur. Mr. King makes me feel old."

"I know exactly how you feel," Joe said.

Katie looked at Joe and shook her head.

"You're just a kid," Arthur said. "It will be a while before you reach my age and a very long while before you reach old age."

Joe smiled. "Yeah, I guess you're right."

"Bonnie said you two are investigating the death of Steven North. You're kind of young to be police detectives."

"We're not. We're more like private investigators," Katie said.

"That's even harder to believe. You two look like you're barely out of high school."

"Thanks, but don't let looks fool you," Katie said. "We are quite competent."

"I'll help you if I can, but I'm not sure how. Steven North crashed his experimental aircraft, and I have no connection with his company. You should be talking to the NTSB."

"We don't need them to tell us what we already know. Someone sabotaged North's plane," Joe said.

"Sabotaged? What makes you think that? The NTSB hasn't released a report yet. I know because I've been following this closely."

"Why are you following it closely if you have no connection?" Joe asked.

"Because his aircraft and ours have many similarities. If his design has a defect, I want to know what it is to ensure we won't have a similar problem."

"His design didn't have a defect," Joe said. "Someone planted a small explosive device that took out his controls."

Arthur's eyes widened. "What? How would you know that? Where did you get your information?"

"I know because I looked inside the plane and saw the hole left by the explosion," Joe said.

"How in the world did you get the authority to look inside that aircraft?"

"We didn't need anyone's permission," Katie said. "We were there. We saw the plane crash. Joe pulled a survivor out of the wreckage."

"Wait a minute. Are you telling me you are private investigators who just happened to witness the very crash that you are investigating?"

"It's a long story," Katie said, "but that is correct. That was part of the reason why we were hired to investigate this."

"Who hired you?" Arthur asked.

"We are not at liberty to tell you that," Joe said.

Arthur leaned back in his chair and said, "Okay, let's assume someone did sabotage North's aircraft. What does that have to do with me?"

"We're here to find out if you did it," Joe said.

Katie looked at Joe, surprised again by his directness.

"Me? You think I would do something so heinous?"

"We don't know. Would you?" Joe asked.

Arthur stood up. "I think you need to leave."

"Please," Katie said. "What my husband is trying to say is we have no idea who is responsible for killing Steven North. We are here trying to eliminate all our potential suspects, starting with you."

Arthur looked at Joe briefly and sat back down. "Okay, fine. Ask me anything."

"We learned you made an offer to buy Zero North," Katie said. "Why?"

Arthur sighed. "Because they are ahead of us in a couple of key areas. Since their aircraft is so similar to ours, if they beat us to market, we could lose a lot of potential customers."

"Wouldn't you agree that sounds like a reason for sabotaging their plane and killing the founder?" Joe asked.

"I can see why you would suspect me, but I don't work that way. I admit that I have a big ego. I want people to recognize me for my accomplishments, but I also want to create something that will help our environment. I would never want to win because the other team didn't show up for the game."

"What about Alan Hutchinson?" Katie asked. "You lured him away from Zero North with more money. Isn't that like cheating?"

"Hell, no. It's what businesses do. It's all part of the game. North was just as capable of hiring my employees away from me or giving his employees more money to stay."

"That would have been difficult since he didn't have anywhere near as much money as you," Katie said.

"That's part of the game, too. You don't enter a poker game without enough money to carry you through a few losses."

"Which key areas are you behind Zero North?" Joe asked.

"Well, they have a unique propeller design that produces about seven percent more thrust than our propellers. They've also found a way to keep the batteries at optimal operating temperatures without adding much weight to the aircraft."

"What are the advantages of your aircraft, compared to theirs?" Katie asked.

"Our main advantage is that our planes will be able to carry four people. Zero North is developing a two-seater. Ours will cost a little more, but we think customers will find us to be a more practical choice."

"For some things," Katie said. "Flight schools or weekend enthusiasts probably don't need four seats. Perhaps your customer base is not as similar to Zero North's as you think."

"Perhaps not now," Arthur agreed, "but I'm sure that if either of our companies makes it big, we will produce several different aircraft versions. They will have a four-seater, and we will have a two-seater. Whichever company is first to market will dominate this niche for years."

"Some people think a little competition is good for both companies," Joe said.

"Some people are idiots," Arthur said. "The only reason a little competition is good, and I stress 'a little,' is because it keeps the government from declaring you a monopoly and imposing price controls. Imagine how much money your power company would make without government restrictions."

"That's true," Joe said, "but without competition, there is no incentive to innovate."

"That makes competition good for the consumer, not necessarily for the business."

"Perhaps we can debate this another time," Katie said. "Do you think we can speak with Alan Hutchinson?"

"Why? Do you think he might be involved in this?"

"We don't know," Joe said, "But whoever placed that explosive device in the plane knew exactly where to put it. That means there is a good chance either Alan Hutchinson or someone who works at Zero North did it. We went to Zero North yesterday but couldn't find anyone with a motive."

"Alan wouldn't have a motive, either. What could he possibly gain from doing something like that?"

"We don't know," Katie said before Joe could say anything. She didn't want to risk Joe saying Arthur might have hired Alan. "We just want to cover all our bases."

"Okay," Arthur said and led them through a door to the factory floor. The place was considerably larger than Zero North's building, but it only had one nearly assembled prototype airplane. It did, however, have an abundant supply of parts.

Arthur led them to the prototype airplane, where two men were working. One man was on his back, his hands inside an open panel. The other man stood next to him, holding a tablet computer. It looked like the screen displayed electrical schematics.

"Alan," Arthur said. "You have a couple of visitors who want to talk to you."

Alan pushed himself out from under the aircraft and stood up. He picked up a towel and wiped his hands. "What is this about?"

"My name is Katie Novak. This is my husband, Joe. We are investigating the death of Steven North. Can you give us a couple of minutes of your time?"

Alan looked at Arthur, who nodded.

Joe looked at Arthur and asked, "Do you mind if we speak to Alan alone?"

Arthur hesitated and said, "Of course. I'll be in my office."

"I don't understand why you would want to talk to me about Steve's death. I mean, I'm sorry he's dead, but I haven't worked there for six months. If that aircraft had a design defect from my time there, someone would have discovered it long before now."

"There were no design defects," Joe said.

Alen looked confused. "So why are you here?"

"Why did you leave Zero North?" Katie asked.

"Money," Alan said. "I got a big raise to come here."

"So, you are motivated by money?" Joe asked.

"Of course, but before you get all judgmental, ask yourselves who isn't motivated by money? I have a family to take care of."

"No one is judging you," Katie said. "We are just here trying to learn the truth about Steven North's death."

"Okay. What do you need to know?"

"If someone wanted to bring down his plane with a very small explosive device, how would they do it?" Joe asked.

"What do you mean by 'very small'? Do you mean like an M80?"

"Something like that, but with a timer," Joe said.

"Well, I guess if you wanted to bring down the plane, it would either have to be inside the instrument panel or at the back of the luggage hold behind the seats. The luggage hold would be easier."

Joe looked at Katie and then back at Alan. "That is precisely what someone did."

"Wait. What? Are you saying someone sabotaged that aircraft?"

"That's exactly what we are saying," Joe said.

"Where were you between Monday afternoon and Tuesday morning?" Joe asked.

"You think I did it? Are you serious? Why would I want to hurt Steve North?"

"For money," Joe said. "You admitted you are motivated by money. You also knew exactly where to plant the explosive."

"I knew where to plant it because I know that aircraft, but so do a dozen people at Zero North. Have you accused any of them?"

Katie looked at Joe, who shrugged. "We're not accusing you, Alan," She said. "We plan on checking everyone out. We spoke with people at Zero North, and coming here seemed like the next logical step."

"Can you tell us where you were between Monday afternoon and Tuesday morning?" Joe repeated.

"I have not been anywhere but here and home all week."

"Can you prove that?" Joe asked.

"Sure, but I don't think I should have to. You're not the police." Alan said.

"You're right," Katie said. "You don't need to prove anything to us, but if you didn't do it and you want to see Steven North's killer brought to justice, we can help do that. We just need to take you off our suspect list so we don't focus too much time on the wrong person."

Alan thought for a moment and said, "Okay, fine. My phone tracks my location." He took out his phone, opened the lock screen, and tapped an icon. He scrolled to the right place and showed Katie and Joe the display. It was a map of his movements on Monday. He then showed them Tuesday's movements.

"Wow, I didn't know there was an app for that," Katie said.

"Every phone has it," Alan said. "You just have to enable it. "I use it partly because I want to be able to show Arthur how many hours I spend here every day, the next time I ask for a raise."

"You could have left your phone at home," Katie said.

Alan sighed and dialed a number on his phone. When it was answered, he put it on speaker. "Hi, Honey. Did I come home after work on Monday?"

"Uh, yeah. Why?"

"Did I stay home all night?"

"Of course. What is this about?"

"I'll explain it when I get home. Thanks."

He hung up and said, "Are you convinced now?"

Katie looked at Joe, who nodded. "We believe you," Katie said. "Can you think of anyone else who might have wanted to hurt Steven North or his company?" Katie asked.

Alan thought momentarily and shook his head. "Sorry. No one comes to mind."

"Okay. Thank you so much for your time."

When they left the building, Katie said, "You were a little hard on him in there."

We needed to know where he was on Monday night. We could have danced around the issue, but eventually, we would have had to ask him."

"I know, but there must be a more subtle way to do it."

"You mean like a poop sandwich?"

"A what?"

"You know. When you sandwich something bad you have to say between two good things. We could have said, 'Alan, we are very impressed with what you are doing here. We want to know if you killed Steven North. And also, what shampoo do you use? Your hair looks great.'"

Katie laughed and shook her head. "You really are something else."

When they got back in the car, Joe asked. "What did you think of Alan?"

"He seemed convincing, but what Scott said about telling someone else where to plant a bomb also seems plausible."

"What about Arthur King?"

"I'm not sure what to think about him," Katie said. "He is motivated by money like Alan Hutchinson, but he is also motivated by prestige, maybe even more so. If he were to get caught committing a crime, he would lose all prestige and respect. He might not want to risk that."

"Many people who commit crimes think they won't get caught. It's unfortunate that you're no longer working at the news station. We could use someone like Billy to research some of these people."

"We can go talk to Bob. Maybe he will let us use him."

"No, I don't think so. He'll want to hire you back."

"Maybe not. Either way, I'd still like to go there while we are in town. I want to see how Ashley's doing."

"Okay, we can go there next."

Chapter 8

After leaving Flight King Aviation, they drove to the Chanel 23 News station. They entered through the employees-only door that led directly to the newsroom. Several people greeted Katie and congratulated her on the birth of the baby. They found Ashley, Katie's friend and former colleague, editing a video at her desk. When she saw Katie, she screamed excitedly and stood to hug her. "Oh my God! Look at you. What are you doing here? It looks like that baby's going to come any minute now."

"Not soon enough," Katie said, putting her hand on her stomach. "Believe it or not, we are investigating another murder."

"No way! In your condition? Are you serious?"

"It seems murders keep finding us," Joe said.

"So, who was murdered this time?"

"A man named Steven North," Katie said. "He ran an aviation startup in West Bend. We saw his plane crash."

"You witnessed a plane crash? Wow! What makes you think he was murdered? Maybe it was a mechanical failure."

"In a nutshell, Joe discovered someone planted an explosive on the plane."

"You guys have become quite the detectives. Who are you investigating this for? I didn't hear you returned to work for the station."

"No. Joe saved one of the crash victims. She recognized me and asked us to investigate."

Ashley touched Joe's arm and said, "Always helping others. I still think you're an angel."

After Joe learned he could use his healing abilities to help others, Ashley was the first person he helped outside of his family and Katie. Someone shot her, leaving her on death's door. At that time, Joe had not yet learned to block people from feeling what he felt, which shocked Ashley when she regained consciousness. She promised to keep Joe's secret and even let him practice on her when he learned how to keep people in the dark as to what he was doing.

She didn't want to lie to her husband, who was told she would not survive the night, so she told him God sent an angel to heal her. She didn't consider it a lie because she had a broad definition of what it meant to be an angel.

They talked for a while, and Katie filled Ashley in on all the details of the case. Ashley then told Katie what had been happening at the station since she left. After a while, Katie said, "I know you need to return to work. We just came to say hello."

"I'm glad you did. I hope you find the killer."

After speaking with Ashley, Katie wanted to say hi to her old boss, Bob, so they went to his office. He invited them in and said, "Katie. Joe. So nice to see you two again. You look much different than the last time I saw you. When's the baby due?"

"Any day now," Katie said.

"So, what brings you to town? Is this where your obstetrician is?"

Katie glanced at Joe and shook her head. "No, we are looking into another murder."

"Seriously? For whom?"

Katie filled Bob in on all the details, and he said, "Wow! I can't believe you two witnessed a plane crash. You know, our station will work with freelance reporters. If you want to report your findings for Channel 23, we'll pay you for it."

"Oh, I hadn't considered that," Katie said. "Okay, that sounds like a win-win. Would I be able to get Billy's help?"

Bob leaned back in his chair and said, "We don't offer his services to other freelancers, and I can't show favoritism. I have a boss to answer to. However, given your service to this station, I think I can allow him to help you if I deduct his time from your pay."

Katie looked at Joe, who smiled and nodded. "That works for us," she said, "especially since we're not in it for the money."

Bob picked up his phone and called Billy. He instructed him to help Katie and Joe in any way he could. Katie thanked him, and they walked to Billy's desk. She wrote a list of names on a sheet of paper and asked him to look into them. They then left the station and returned to Katie's car.

"Maybe we should say hi to Gabe before we return to the hotel," Katie said.

"That's a good idea," Joe said. "Then we can go to the art museum."

Katie hesitated. "Oh, uh, yeah. Sure."

Joe looked at Katie. "You don't want to go, do you?"

"I have mixed feelings, but we should go. Your photographs are on display at an art museum. I would be a bad wife if I didn't go to see them. Besides, I've seen dead people before. I can handle it."

"Why don't you call Gabe? Maybe he can meet us there," Joe said.

"That's a good idea." Katie pushed a button on her steering wheel and said, "Call Gabe."

Gabe picked up the call on the second ring. "Hi, Katie. How are you?"

"Hi, Gabe. Joe and I are in town, and we learned this morning that Joe's photos from the war will be at the art museum. We're heading there now and thought you might want to join us if you can get some time off for lunch."

"I would love to see Joe's photographs. I'll meet you there shortly. I want to pick up Carmen on the way."

Gabe knew Joe's secret. Several months earlier, as Joe recovered from getting shot in the back, Gabe started questioning his resilience. It was the third potentially fatal injury Joe had recovered from in three months. It didn't help that Katie accidentally mentioned that Joe was in the army and served in Africa. Gabe had Joe checked out and learned he had changed his identity. As a police captain, that information put Gabe in an awkward position. He couldn't ignore what he learned. That forced Joe to show Gabe his healing powers to prove he wasn't hiding from the law. Gabe promised to keep his secret, and he kept his word. He didn't even tell his wife.

***

When they arrived at the museum, they waited in the car until Gabe and his wife, Carmen, arrived. They all greeted each other warmly. "It is so nice to see you two again," Carmen said. To Katie, she said, "I can't believe how beautiful you look. When I was that pregnant, I looked like a walrus."

"I find that hard to believe," Katie said.

"Believe it. People would throw fish at me."

"Don't listen to her," Gabe said. "She was beautiful from the beginning of her pregnancies until the end."

Carmen leaned against Gabe and smiled. "You are such a liar. Thank you."

After going inside, they followed the signs to the World War II exhibit. This led them to a large room with hundreds of photographs on display. Many hung on the walls, and many more were displayed on temporary dividers in the center of the room. Joe's photos were displayed on the largest wall in the back of the room, as well as half of the wall to the right.

In the center of the back wall hung a plaque with his name, Joe Young, and a little of his history. It stated that he was injured in combat but survived and went on to become a successful photographer after the war. It also said he died in 1982 at 66 years old. Katie felt oddly uncomfortable reading about Joe's death, even though she knew it was not correct.

Katie knew Joe had changed his identity several times to hide the fact that he didn't age. Still, she never discussed with him how and when he had done so. 1982 was when he and his wife bought the resort, so she assumed moving to a new location was the perfect time to change his identity since nobody knew him by his previous name.

Cynthia was talking to a few people on the other side of the room when she noticed Katie and Joe. She approached them and said, "Hi, Katie. Hi, Joe. I'm so glad you could join us. Your donation was so generous. Your grandfather's photos have gotten so much attention already."

"I'm happy to put them to good use," Joe said.

Carmen's mouth hung open in awe as she looked at Joe's photographs. Some were photos of men and their machines, but many were of death and destruction. "How awful!" she finally said.

"They are awful," Gabe agreed. "That must have been a terrible experience for, uh, your great-grandfather, Joe."

"Yes. I'm sure he was happy to come home."

"By the way, Cynthia," Katie said, "these are our friends, Gabe and Carmen."

They shook hands, and Cynthia said, "I'm pleased to meet you both."

After discussing the photos for a few minutes, Cynthia excused herself and spoke with other visitors. Katie then looked closer at all of Joe's photographs. The first time she saw his war photos, they disturbed her so much that she quickly closed the book after looking at only a few. Now, she studied them, wondering what was going through Joe's mind when he took those photographs. She tried to imagine herself in the same situation, but couldn't fathom it.

"I hadn't thought too much about it until now, Joe, but I really respect your grandfather and every other soldier who fought in that war, or any war for that matter," Katie said. "I would have been a basket case after day one."

"I think people don't realize how strong they are until they face a life-or-death challenge," Joe said. "I see you as a fighter. Don't forget, the last time you were kidnapped, you handled it better than I did."

"I guess you're right. By the second kidnapping, it starts to seem normal."

Joe looked at Katie. "I hope you are joking right now."

"Of course, I'm joking. It takes at least three kidnappings before it starts to seem normal."

Joe shook his head and looked at Gabe and Carmen. "I noticed the museum has a café. Is anyone hungry for lunch?"

Everyone agreed, so they ate lunch at the café. Gabe and Carmen returned to work after eating, while Katie and Joe returned to their hotel.

In the car, on the way to the hotel, Katie said, "I noticed the plaque at the museum said Joe Young died at 66 years old. Was that the first time you changed your identity?"

"Yeah. Can you believe I passed for 66? I didn't know how to change my identity much before then. Shortly before Marie and I bought the cabin, we met a man while camping. He and his wife were big drinkers, and he talked too much while drunk. He bragged about quitting his corporate job and making twice as much money on the side doing half the work. After some pressing, he admitted that people hired him to hack into computer systems. I asked if he could change someone's identity, and he said it was a piece of cake. That was back before the internet was a thing. Anyway, I kept in touch, and when we bought the resort, I called him. Not only did he give me a new identity, but Joe Young got an official death certificate."

"I can't believe we never talked about this before. How did you pass for 66 years old?"

"It wasn't easy. I learned how to use prosthetics from a makeup artist. It gave me the appearance of wrinkles next to my eyes. They used to call them crow's feet. I also colored my hair."

"What name did you take back then?"

"I became John Joseph Young. The youngest son of my oldest son. I had to pretend to be Marie's grandson in public."

"That must have felt awkward."

"Yes, it did sometimes, but at least I could still go by 'Joe' most of the time. Marie and I just had to be careful not to show any affection when people were around."

"What about the next time you changed your name?"

"That was when I went back to Josip Novak. It was in 2002, shortly after Marie died."

"Wait a minute. Your driver's license says you were born in 1996. That means you were six years old in 2002."

"Originally, my birthday was in 1984, but my hacker friend changed it for me years later. He died shortly after he did that, so I don't know how I will change it next time."

"Didn't your hacker friend notice that you were staying young?"

"I paid him a lot of money for his service. He didn't ask any questions, and I didn't volunteer any information. Besides, he was breaking the law. Who would he tell?"

"I hadn't really thought about it, but twenty years from now, we might both have to start over again."

Joe took Katie's hand in his. "We will worry about that when the time comes, although we should probably start making friends with computer hackers."

"You mean like Billy?"

"Yes, but more shady."

***

Once back at the hotel, Katie removed her jacket, kicked her shoes off, and sprawled out on the bed. "Ahhhhh."

"Are you okay?" Joe asked.

"I'm fine. I just need to rest. I can't wait until this baby comes, so I won't always feel so tired."

"Um, about that," Joe said. "I wouldn't get your hopes up."

Katie sat up and moved over so Joe could sit next to her. "If you are going to tell me the baby will keep us up at night, I already know that. I also know that you will be there to help out."

"Oh, no," Joe said. "Taking care of a baby is women's work."

Katie slapped Joe on the arm, and Joe laughed. "I know you're trying to be funny, but it's not working," she said.

Joe leaned over and kissed Katie. "Of course, I will help take care of little Joey. In fact, I'm looking forward to it. It's been over eighty years since I had a baby to care for, other than an occasional grandchild."

"Are you nervous at all? I mean, eighty years is a long time. Are you worried you might have forgotten how to care for a baby?"

"I remember when my first son was born. I had no idea what I was doing. I was afraid to hold him. He seemed so fragile. That fear was also there when my other two children were born, and I'm sure I will have that same fear when Joey is born. Fortunately, they grow fast and become strong. Soon, you forget what in the world you were afraid of."

"I think I will be nervous until they move out and get married."

Joe laughed. "That soon, huh? I still worry about Susan."

Katie put her head on Joe's shoulder and said, "I hope when Joey's eighty, we will still be here worrying about him."

Joe kissed Katie on her head. "I hope so, too."

Katie's phone beeped. She realized it was still in her coat pocket and asked Joe to get it for her. When he returned with the phone, she saw the message was from Billy. "It looks like Billy sent us the information we asked for."

"What does it say?" Joe asked.

"Let's look at it on my laptop. Can you bring it to me?"

Joe retrieved Katie's laptop and handed it to her. She opened her email program and found the message from Billy. It contained several attachments. She opened the first one. "It says Steven North was nearly broke. Other than his company, he had no other investments. He took out a second mortgage on his house, and at the time of his death, he had only sixteen hundred dollars in the bank. It also says he had a one-million-dollar life insurance policy."

"Well, at least his family will be okay financially," Joe said.

"Maybe it was suicide," Katie suggested. "He had almost no money. He was heavily in debt, and his company was nearly bankrupt. Maybe he thought killing himself would be the only way he could provide for his family."

"That is certainly a possibility. Insurance companies won't pay for suicides, but if he made it look like an accident or even murder, his wife would be assured of a payout. My only issue with that idea is that, from everything we've heard about Steven North, he doesn't seem like the kind of guy who would let someone else die with him."

"I suppose you're right," Katie said. After a few seconds, she added, "Sonia told us she surprised Steve when she showed up at the hangar and insisted he take her with him. Maybe he had already set the timer on the explosive and couldn't back out."

Joe thought momentarily and shook his head slightly. "I don't know. Maybe. It just seems a little cold-blooded. I suppose he could have been a psychopath and was good at manipulating others, but psychopaths don't commit suicide for their family's benefit."

"What about his wife? If their relationship was on the rocks, she might have opted to get rid of him for the million dollars."

"Is there anything about her in there?"

"No, not specifically about her. These are joint financial records."

"We should talk to their neighbors tomorrow," Joe said. "Maybe someone can tell us what kind of relationship they had. Who's next on the list?"

Katie opened another attachment. "Next is Arthur King. He has a net worth of a little over two billion dollars."

"That's a lot of money. How could anyone spend it all?"

"I guess you could use it to start new businesses, like Flight King Aviation."

"Good point. How much did he invest in that business?"

"So far, he has invested almost fifty million dollars into it."

"Wow. It's a wonder he hasn't surpassed Zero North by now."

"You need more than money," Katie said. "Arthur King may be great at developing video games, but he doesn't understand airplanes like Stephen North did."

"That makes sense. What else does it say about him?"

"Well, he's married with two children. He has a sixteen-year-old daughter and a nineteen-year-old son. The son is away at Northwestern University."

"Does his wife work?"

"She does. She's a chiropractor and has her own practice. She obviously doesn't need the money, so she must love what she does."

"I guess so, or she wants a reason to leave the house."

"Since her husband goes to the office, the only advantage to leaving the house is to get away from the kids. Oh, wow! Are kids really that troublesome?"

"I think we're getting ahead of ourselves. She probably just loves her job."

Katie nodded. "Yeah. I'm sure that's it. Anyway, next on the list is Alan Hutchinson. He is married with three kids, all under seven years old."

"I can see why he needed more money," Joe said. "What does it say about his finances?"

"He has twenty-one thousand dollars in his retirement fund and around five thousand dollars in savings. His checking account has only a few hundred dollars, but he has ten thousand dollars worth of crypto. Nothing indicates he received a large sum of money recently."

"What's crypto?" Joe asked.

"It's like imaginary money that has real value. You wouldn't understand. I barely understand it."

"Well, I don't think we can scratch Alan off our list yet, but he should be near the bottom. I'm not sure, but I also don't think Arthur King was involved unless he recruited someone who currently works at Zero North. However, that seems unlikely."

"I agree. It was probably someone still employed at Zero North, but I can't imagine what anyone would gain by torpedoing the company."

"I don't know either. We are obviously missing something. What does that report say about Larry Cooper?"

Katie looked at the screen and scrolled down. "It says he is also married with two children, both grown and away at college. His wife is a high school English teacher. He has an MBA from Harvard."

"That's impressive," Joe said. "Where did he work prior to Zero North?"

Katie looked at her screen and said, "He was the Executive Assistant to the Chief Operating Officer at United Airlines."

"Oh, so he has industry experience," Joe said. "Going from a large airline to a small start-up aircraft manufacturer must be quite a change. Working for a large company probably taught him the art of climbing the corporate ladder by backstabbing the competition. Maybe killing Steven North was a way to reach the top rung of the ladder."

Katie looked at Joe and shook her head. "You've grown quite cynical in your old age. I don't think he was motivated by advancement. It says his wife was born right here in West Bend. Maybe she wanted to settle down in her hometown, and he was willing to make her happy by taking this job. It is exactly what I did for you."

"I see your point. If that's true, maybe his wife and family come first. What else does that report say about him?"

Well, he and his wife have over five hundred thousand dollars in their retirement account, eleven thousand dollars in savings, and another twenty-five hundred dollars in their checking account. Besides their retirement account, their only investment is in Zero North."

"It sounds like they have done very well. Have there been any large deposits recently?"

"No. Nothing out of the ordinary."

"How much did they invest in Zero North?"

"It says he invested fifty thousand dollars into the company. That's a lot of money to lose. If he killed Steven North to get control of the company, that would be a risky move."

"If he felt North was running the company into the ground, he might have thought getting rid of him was the only chance to save the company," Joe suggested.

"I suppose," Katie said, "but if Steve's flight to Minneapolis was successful, that alone might have saved the company."

"I don't know. Maybe Cooper didn't know the reason for the trip. Or maybe he's in league with Arthur King. Maybe if King buys Zero North, Larry will get a cushy job and a share of Flight King Aviation. Can Billy find phone records for us?"

"He's very resourceful. I bet he can."

"Ask him if Arthur King called or received calls from anyone at Zero North besides Steven North."

Katie typed a message to Billy and sent it off.

"Who's next?" Joe asked.

"Next is our home wrecker, Elena Petrova."

"She hasn't wrecked anyone's home."

"Not yet, but it won't be long before Sonia finds out what Scott is doing."

"We don't know what he's doing. It could be innocent flirting."

"Flirting is not innocent."

"Maybe not, but it's also not cheating. Can we focus less on domestic affairs and more on the murder investigation?"

"Okay, fine. Elena Petrova is twenty-eight years old. She's never been married and rents an apartment here in West Bend. She has no investments or retirement savings but has twenty-five thousand dollars in her savings account."

"Is that recent?" Joe asked.

Billy sent several attachments, including bank records. Katie clicked on the one for Elena. She scrolled down and said, "It looks like she built up her savings gradually. There is nothing to indicate she did something bad for money."

"Are you disappointed?"

Katie looked at Joe. "Do you think that I'm so petty that I would want to see her go to jail for being a home wrecker?"

"No. I don't think you are petty, but in this case, I would understand if you felt that way."

There was a brief pause, and Katie said, "Actually, I do wish she were our bad guy. Does that make me a bad person?"

"No. It just makes you human. Who's next?"

"Next is Max Allen. He is thirty-one years old. He divorced a little over a year ago. He owns a home here in West Bend. His seven-year-old daughter lives with her mother in Milwaukee. He pays five hundred dollars per month for child support. He also has no retirement savings, but invested five thousand dollars in Zero North. He has about six hundred dollars in his checking and another four thousand in savings."

"So far, none of this is helpful. I don't see anything that looks unusual."

"Maybe everyone is innocent. Maybe one of the lower-level employees did it," Katie suggested.

"I doubt it. No one else knew the codes to get into the hangar."

"I don't know. Perhaps we should do something to take our minds off the case for a while. Sometimes, it helps to take a short break."

"Okay, Katie. What would you like to do?"

"I don't know. Let's take a walk. We can check out downtown West Bend. It's not far from here."

"Are you sure you are up to it?"

"I don't know, Joe, but I don't want to sit around here."

***

They put on their coats and went outside. A light snow fell as they walked to the Milwaukee River. As they crossed the bridge, a crisp breeze carried the scent of burning wood from a nearby chimney. Below them, ice clung to the banks of the river while water flowed freely down the center. At their location, the river wasn't wide. It was more like a stream.

They were in the downtown area shortly after reaching the other side of the bridge. They had seen it when they arrived in town. It looked like a typical small town with many one-story and two-story brick buildings. With snow on the ground, it had a charm like those small towns depicted in many Christmas movies.

They walked past several stores, and Joe looked at Katie, surprised. "Are you not interested in shopping?"

Katie slapped Joe's arm. "Really? Do you think I wanted to come here to shop?"

"Well, it wouldn't be unheard of."

Katie laughed. "I'm teasing you, Joe. Of course, I want to shop, but haven't yet found what I'm looking for."

"What are you looking for?"

"I'll tell you when I see it."

They walked for another minute, and then Katie saw it. She pointed ahead and to the left. "There it is."

They crossed the street and entered a children's clothing store. "We already bought a boatload of clothes for the baby," Joe said.

"Yes, but we brought none of it with us. What if we are still here when the baby is born?"

"I'm sure Michael or Eric would happily bring us some of the baby's clothes."

"I'm sure they would, too, but I want little Joey's first outfit to be special. If he is born here, I want his clothing to be from here, too."

"Okay. If that's how you feel, we should find something special for him."

They looked through the store until Katie found something she liked. She picked it up to show Joe. "Look. It has dinosaurs on it. Were dinosaurs still around when you were little?"

"Very funny. You are just asking for it, young lady."

Katie laughed. "I think we should get him this one."

After leaving the store, Katie saw a coffee shop and said, "Let's take a break and have a coffee."

"You know I'm not a coffee drinker, Katie."

"I got you a coffee with heavy cream once, and you liked it. Maybe they can make it like that here."

"Liked is a strong word. I found it acceptable."

"Just humor me."

"Okay, but in your condition, I don't like you drinking more than one cup of coffee per day."

"Relax. The coffee at the hotel isn't very good. I barely touched mine this morning."

As they stood in line to order, Katie said, "It's almost dinnertime. Would you like to get a sandwich while we're here?"

Joe agreed, and Katie ordered two coffees with heavy cream and two sandwiches. They sat next to each other near a window. Across the street was a bar. They watched people walk in and out of the bar while they ate and sipped their coffee. The snow had picked up, and Joe said, "We should probably head back."

Joe stood up and put a hand out for Katie, but a group of people walking into the bar caught her attention. He looked out the window at what she was looking at. They saw several men and women walk into the bar, most of whom they recognized from Zero North, including Max, Scott, and Elena. Scott and Elena walked in last, with Scott holding the door open for Elena.

Katie's jaw hung open before saying, "Oh, my God! Did you see that? That bastard lied. He said the women do their own thing."

"Relax, Katie. If he were cheating, he wouldn't be with a group."

"If he's not cheating, why would he lie?"

"I don't know. Women can be jealous. Maybe he didn't want his wife to read too much into it."

"Women are jealous because men are pigs."

"Really? Is that what you think?"

"Well, maybe not all men, but some definitely."

Joe studied Katie's face and asked. "Were you hurt by a man in that way?"

Katie shook her head. "I don't want to talk about it. Let's go back to the hotel."

When they got back to their hotel room, Katie said, "I'm sorry, Joe. I know all men aren't bad. I know I can trust you. I just don't understand why so many men can't be happy with what they have."

"It's not just men. I have known many men whom women have hurt."

Katie sat on the bed and sighed. "I know. People who aren't happy should talk about it instead of cheating. That's just hurtful."

Joe sat next to Katie and put an arm around her. "Did someone cheat on you?"

After a long pause, Katie said, "Jimmy Anderson. I dated him during my senior year of high school. I thought we had a future together, but I didn't count on Eva Radcliffe. Apparently, a nice set of boobs trumps an intelligent woman with high ambitions."

"What are you talking about? You have nice boobs."

Katie looked at Joe and put her hand on his cheek. "Thank you for being nice, but I know they are just average."

"Are you kidding? That Jimmy guy was an idiot. Your boobs are perfect for your body, and your body is perfect. Everything is in the exact right proportion. Even now, at almost nine months pregnant, you look beautiful. Honestly, I'm glad you dated an idiot in high school. If not, we might have never met."

Katie kissed Joe. "I'm glad about that, too."

They kissed again. Soon, it became passionate, and Katie pushed Joe down and lay next to him. She kissed him again and put her head on his chest. "Did I tell you today how much I love you?"

Chapter 9

Katie and Joe drove to Steven North's house after breakfast the following morning. They learned from Michael that Helen North and her children were still checked in at the resort, but he expected them to leave later that day. Katie and Joe felt it best to talk to the neighbors while Helen was away.

When they turned onto the street, Joe noticed how different the left side was from the right. It was as if one neighborhood ended and another began. On the left were several older, two-story homes that sat very close together. There were no driveways in front of the homes, but an alley ran behind them.

On the right side of the road stood larger homes set farther apart and farther from the street. These homes had driveways and garages. Helen North's home was a beautiful, Tudor-style home. It wasn't huge by any means, but it was attractive and nicely landscaped. Joe guessed it had at least three bedrooms, probably four. To the right was a large empty lot. To the left was an equally nice home, possibly a little bigger, but with a detached garage. Katie parked between the two homes, and they both got out of the car and looked around.

"What do you think?" Katie asked.

"I think if anyone knows them, it would be the people to the left."

"My thoughts exactly."

The house was on a small hill, so Katie and Joe walked up the stepped sidewalk. It looked like someone had shoveled it after the last snow, but it had patches of ice, so Joe held Katie's arm as they walked to the front door. Katie rang the bell, and they waited. A teenage boy answered the door, and Katie asked, "Is your mom or dad here?"

The boy turned around and yelled, "Mom! Door!" He then walked away, leaving the door half open.

Ten seconds later, a middle-aged woman came to the door. She wore a floral-patterned skirt and a pink sweater. Her medium-length brown hair was tied behind her head with a ribbon. She looked surprised to see someone she didn't know and said, "Oh, hi. Can I help you?"

"Hi. I'm Katie, and this is Joe. We are investigating the death of Steven North."

The woman shook her head. "Oh, that was a terrible accident. I'm just heartbroken over it. Are you folks with the NTSB or whatever you call it?"

"No, ma'am. We are private investigators," Katie said.

"Private investigators? Really? Did Helen hire you?"

"We are not at liberty to disclose our client," Joe said. "Can you answer a few questions for us?"

"Of course, but I don't know how I can help."

"Did you know Steve and Helen North well?" Katie asked.

"What do you mean by 'did?' Is Helen okay?"

"Helen is fine," Katie said. "I mean, as a couple. Did you visit them at their home? How did they treat each other?"

"What kind of investigation is this? What does that have to do with Steve's accident?"

"We don't believe it was an accident," Joe said. "We believe someone sabotaged his airplane."

The woman's mouth hung open. "What? Are you serious?"

"Yes," Joe said. "Can you tell us about Steve and Helen's relationship?"

The woman hesitated momentarily and said, "Well, if you're looking for dirt, you won't get it from me. I never saw a better relationship. I wish my husband and I got along as well as they did."

"So you never witnessed any big fights between them?" Katie asked.

"Hell no. They would sometimes playfully tease each other, but were obviously in love. Helen once complained that she wished Steve would work less, but she knew he was trying to get his business off the ground and was very supportive of him."

Katie looked at Joe and then back at the woman. "Are you aware of anyone they didn't get along with? Perhaps a disgruntled neighbor."

"No. I haven't heard of any disputes with neighbors. They weren't the kind of people who caused problems for others, and, as far as I know, none of our neighbors caused any problems for them."

"Okay," Katie said. "Thank you so much for your time."

When they were back in the car, Katie said, "I think we can eliminate Helen North as a suspect."

"I agree. If what she says is true, it's also unlikely either was cheating on the other."

Katie's phone beeped. She checked it and saw a message from Billy. "It's from Billy. He says Arthur King's phone records don't show any calls to numbers in West Bend except a call three weeks ago to Zero North."

"That must have been when he contacted Steve North about buying his company. It looks like we are back to square one."

"More like square zero," Katie said as she started the car and pulled away.

"I think we need to establish a timeline. Can you call Sonia?"

Katie dialed Sonia's number. When she answered, Katie said, "Hi, Sonia. Joe would like to ask you a couple of questions."

"Hi, Joe. What's up?"

"Hi, Sonia. We need to know when Steve North decided to fly to Minneapolis." Joe said.

"I don't know when he made the decision. He didn't mention it to me before I left for the day. Scott worked late and told me when he got home."

"What time was that?" Joe asked

"I think it was around eight."

"I think I know what Joe's getting at," Katie said. "If we can learn when exactly he decided to fly, we can assume the person who planted the explosive did so after that time."

"That makes sense, but I don't know when he decided to make the trip. He said nothing to me before I left work. When I showed up the next morning at the hangar, he made it clear he didn't want me there. The timing of his decision didn't seem important then."

"If he didn't want you there, he wouldn't have told Scott either. How did he know?" Joe asked.

"I don't know. He didn't mention that. Maybe he learned it from someone else there."

"Is Scott nearby?" Katie asked.

"No. He's picking up a part from one of our suppliers. If you want to know when Steve decided to fly to Minneapolis, check with the airport. He probably would have filed a flight plan right away."

"That's a good idea," Joe said. "One more thing. Did you check with the alarm company about when the alarm was deactivated?"

"Oh, shoot. I'm sorry. With everything that has been going on, I forgot. I will look into that right away."

"Thanks, Sonia," Katie said. "Text me the times when you find out."

***

When they hung up with Sonia, they drove to the airport. They parked in a small lot and walked to the main building. Inside, they saw a middle-aged woman behind a counter and decided she was the person they should talk to. They approached the counter, and Katie said, "Good morning. I'm Katie, and this is Joe. We are private investigators looking into the death of Steven North."

"Oh, yes," the woman said. "That was a real tragedy. Everyone here knew Steve. He was very well-liked around here."

"We're sorry for your loss," Joe said. "We know he filed a flight plan before his flight. We'd like to know what time he filed it."

"Of course," the woman said. "Just a moment." She walked into an office behind her.

A few moments later, she returned, followed by a middle-aged man. He was around fifty, of average build, with thinning hair cut very short. He said, "Hi. I'm Matthew Ellison, the airport manager. How can I help you?"

"Hi, Mr. Ellison. I'm Katie, and this is Joe. We are investigating the death of Steven North."

"Yes. Sarah mentioned that. His crash was a real shame. It's unfortunate, but accidents sometimes happen with experimental aircraft. Until the NTSB releases its report, it seems like there's nothing to investigate."

"The NTSB is taking its time, but we know the plane was sabotaged," Joe said.

"Sabotaged? How would you know that?"

"In a nutshell, we witnessed the crash," Joe said. "I examined the damage. Someone planted a small explosive device in a critical area."

Ellison took a step back and slowly shook his head. "That's unbelievable. Who would want to kill Steve?"

"That's what we want to find out," Katie said. "Do you know anyone who would want to hurt him? Was he feuding with anyone?"

"No, no. Absolutely not. Everyone liked and respected Steve North."

"What about his company?" Katie asked. "Could anyone have wanted to see his company fail?"

"I doubt it. Everyone here was rooting for him. We were hoping Zero North would become the next Tesla. I know that's unrealistic, but that would have put West Bend on the map."

"The person who planted the explosive probably did so after he filed his flight plan," Joe said. "Can you tell us what time that was?"

"Sure. Just a minute." Ellison logged into the computer at the counter. After about fifteen seconds, he said, "He filed his flight plan just before five on Monday afternoon."

"Thanks so much for your help," Katie said.

When they left the building, Joe said, "I'd like to see Zero North's hangar again. Do you think you can walk that far?"

"Honestly, Joe, I feel like I need to sit down. Can we drive there?"

"Of course, my dear."

They got in Katie's car and drove around to Zero North's hangar. Katie didn't bother parking in the parking lot. She just stopped near the back door of the hangar. Joe said, "You can wait here. I just want to check something out."

"No. I'm coming with you," Katie said as she opened her door.

Joe scanned the area. There was a hangar on both sides of Zero North's hangar, and several hangars were across the road. After a few seconds, Joe pointed to a hangar across the road and two down. "Let's check that out," he said.

They returned to the car, and Katie drove forward until they reached the hangar. They got out of the car again, and Joe pointed to the top of the building. A security camera sat in each corner, pointing at the center from opposite directions. One pointed toward Zero North's Hangar. Katie smiled. "Just like Veteran's Park," she said, referring to a camera that helped them crack their first case.

"That's right," Joe said. "This one is a little farther away. Hopefully, we will get something useful from it."

"My fingers are crossed," Katie said.

The main door was closed. Joe checked the side door. It was locked. The sign on the building read, "WB Aerial Photography." The sign included a phone number that Joe asked Katie to call.

Katie called the number and got a recording. She left a message and hung up. "There was no answer," she said. "Perhaps they are out taking pictures."

"I guess we'll have to wait," Joe said.

"Let's take a break. Maybe we can have lunch. I'm getting hungry."

They headed back to the downtown area and had lunch at the same restaurant where they had breakfast when they arrived in town. While they were eating, Katie's phone beeped. She checked it and said, "It's a text from Sonia."

"What's it say?" Joe asked.

"It says someone deactivated the alarm at seven forty-five and reactivated it at seven-fifty."

"Interesting," Joe said. "Didn't Sonia say that Scott got home from work that night around eight?"

"Oh, my God! Are you suggesting that Scott did this?"

"The timing fits."

Katie paused for a moment and slowly shook her head. "I can't believe I'm defending the guy, but Sonia said he got home around eight." She stressed the word "around." "The drive from the airport to their house is at least ten minutes. If he got home before eight, the timing wouldn't work."

"Maybe we can ask her if she's sure about the time."

Katie shook her head. "We can't do that. That would be the same as calling her husband a murderer to her face."

"What do you suggest then?"

"I don't know. What motive would Scott have for killing Steven North?"

Joe shook his head. "None that I can think of."

"So, maybe it's just a coincidence."

"Coincidence or not, we need to keep Scott Wilson on our radar."

When they finished lunch and returned to the car, Katie said, "I'm not sure what we should do now."

"Let's forget about the case for a while. We should visit the local hospital."

"That's a good idea, Joe. We can look for someone to heal."

"No. That's not why. I worry we will still be in town when the baby comes. I want to set you up at the hospital just in case."

"What do I need a hospital for when I have a healer for a husband?"

"You're joking, right?"

"Maybe a little, but you delivered a baby before. You can handle it."

"I delivered a baby once with your help. This time, you will not be in a position to help."

"Now it's you that must be joking. It seems to me I will be the one doing all the work."

"You know what I mean. Assisting with childbirth is best left to the professionals."

"Okay, Joe. I agree with you. Let's go check out the hospital."

Chapter 10

They drove to the hospital, which was on the edge of town. They spent a lot of time in Milwaukee hospitals several months earlier, after first Ashley was shot and then Joe. Unlike the towering hospitals in Milwaukee, this one had fewer floors but was more spread out. Land was obviously cheaper on the edge of West Bend compared to the center of Milwaukee.

They parked in the main lot and walked inside. Once inside, they walked straight ahead to the main desk. A man was helping a patient to the right, so they stepped up to the left side of the counter. A woman smiled and asked, "Can I help you?"

"We are visiting from out of town," Joe said. "As you can see, my wife is close to giving birth. If that happens before we go home, we want to be prepared."

"I understand," the woman said, handing them a clipboard and a pen. "Please fill this out, and we will pre-register you."

"Katie and Joe sat and filled out the forms and then returned them to the woman at the front desk. She looked through them and said, "We need your doctor's contact information."

Katie looked at Joe and then back at the woman. "We don't have a doctor."

The woman looked confused. "What do you mean? You have no doctor, or you don't have an obstetrician?"

"I don't have a doctor or an obstetrician," Katie said.

"Oh, my!" the woman said. "As far along as you are, you need to have a doctor."

"We live in a rural area," Joe said. "There are no doctors in town."

"I've been seeing what you would call a 'natural healer,'" Katie said.

The woman wrote something on a piece of paper and handed it to Katie. "I'll get you in the system, but you should see a real doctor as soon as possible. Here's the number to a local obstetrician. Give her a call." She looked at her watch. "You probably can't get in today, but maybe you can make an appointment for Monday."

When they walked away, Joe said, "What did she mean by a 'real' doctor?"

"Don't take it personally, Joe. These days, people trained in the medical field don't consider natural medicine legitimate."

"Not long before I was born, natural medicine was highly regarded until the rise of the pharmaceutical industry. Suddenly, drugs were the answer to everything because herbs were not profitable."

Katie looked at Joe and shook her head. "You really are quite the cynic."

"Eighty years from now, you will be, too."

"I hate to admit it, but you're probably right."

"Maybe while we are at the hospital, we can look for someone to heal."

"I'd like that, Joe. I just don't know how often we can get away with pretending we are religious zealots. We were lucky the last couple of times, but what if the patient is an atheist? They're not going to let us hold hands while we pray for them."

"That's a good point. Maybe I can pretend to be a reflexologist like I did with Cynthia."

"I've heard of that but don't know exactly what it is."

"I don't fully understand it either, but it has something to do with qi."

"What's qi?"

"The Chinese believe it is like an energy force that flows through all living things."

"You mean like The Force?"

Joe laughed. "Yes, but without the lightsabers. Anyway, they believe illness is caused by your qi being blocked, and massaging the hands or feet can unblock it."

"Do you believe it?"

"I don't know. There are a lot of different causes of illnesses, but I can see it working in some cases, perhaps many cases."

"Okay, I think it's worth a shot."

They walked back to the counter. This time, the woman who helped them was busy, but the man was free. Joe asked him, "Can you tell us what room Mary Smith is in?"

The man checked his computer and said, "She's in room 212." He pointed to the left. Just take the elevator to the second floor."

Katie looked surprised but said nothing until they reached the elevator and Joe pressed the button. "How did you know there was a Mary Smith here?"

"I didn't. I just played the odds. Mary Smith was the most common name I could think of."

"I need to take you to Vegas."

Katie dropped the business card the woman gave her in the trash before they got on the elevator. When they reached the second floor, they quickly found room 212. A woman, perhaps sixty-five, lay on the bed while a man around the same age sat beside her. They walked inside, and Joe said, "Hi. I'm sorry for the interruption. My name is Joe, and this is my wife, Katie. I'm a reflexologist, and we like to volunteer our free time to help people. Do you mind if I ask what's wrong?"

The woman looked at the man, who said, "What the hell is a reflexologist?"

"Well, I guess you can think of me as somewhere between a massage therapist and an acupuncturist."

"My wife was just diagnosed with lung cancer. Your voodoo therapies are not going to help her."

The woman reached out and touched her husband's arm. "Relax, Henry. They only want to help." She looked at Katie and Joe and said, "I'm Mary, and this is my husband, Henry. He's just trying to protect me."

"We understand," Katie said. "If you don't want our help, that's fine, but you should know my husband is a miracle worker. If he can't help you, nobody can."

"How can you help?" Mary asked.

"If you give me your hand, I can show you," Joe said.

Mary looked at Harry, who slowly nodded. "Okay," she said and held out her hand.

Joe took her hand and randomly pressed areas on her palm. He quickly connected to her and felt where the cancer had invaded her lungs. "There are pressure points in your hand that can unblock your qi," he said.

"What is qi?" Mary asked.

"It is energy. Some call it a life force."

Henry shook his head but said nothing.

Joe stopped talking and concentrated on his task. Instead of one large tumor, there were many small tumors. That made his job more difficult because he needed to cut the blood supply to each and every tumor. If he missed one, it would survive and possibly spread. After a little more than ten minutes, he felt he had gotten every last tumor. He let go and said, "I think you will be okay now. Give it a week and have the doctors rescan you before you start any treatments."

"I hope you're right," Mary said. "Have you treated people with cancer before?"

"Only once," Joe said. "I treated a woman with breast cancer."

"Did it work?" Mary asked.

"It's been about eight months, and the last time I checked, she was cancer-free."

"That's wonderful," Mary said. "Do you have a business card? If it works, I would happily tell people about you."

"I appreciate that, Mary," Joe said, "but we don't do this for profit."

***

When they left the hospital, Katie said, "It still amazes me that you can heal someone with cancer so quickly."

"Cancer is easy. Healing from someone hitting you with their car is the real challenge."

Katie rolled her eyes. "Are you ever going to let it go? I said I was sorry like a hundred times."

"I'm sorry, Honey, but it's the only thing I have to tease you about. That and your little toy of a car."

They reached Katie's car just as Joe made his comment. Katie opened her door and looked over the car at Joe. "Don't you make fun of my beautiful car!" She loved her little Mini Cooper and didn't like Joe making fun of it, even though she knew he was kidding.

Joe laughed as he got in the car. "Okay. You know I'm kidding. I actually like your little car. My last car was a Lincoln Town Car. Technically, it was Marie's car, but I drove it sometimes. I hated trying to squeeze that thing into parking spots."

"Why was that your last car?" Katie asked.

I told you I was a wreck after Marie died. I rarely left the cabin and certainly didn't need a car, so I gave it to Michael. Several years later, he gave it to Eric."

"Do you mean that big boat Eric drives is your car?"

"Yes. He and Michael kept it in good condition."

So how did you get groceries without a car?"

Michael or Susan sometimes took me to the grocery store or bought me food when they shopped for themselves. When Eric got his driver's license, he was happy to have a reason to drive somewhere, so I would go to the store with him. It was a good excuse to spend time with my great-grandson.

"Now you have me to take you to the grocery store," Katie said. "Speaking of that, after the baby is born, you will have to go shopping without me for a while."

"Really? I thought you didn't trust me with your car."

"I don't trust you with my car, so you better be careful."

"Are you kidding? You know me."

"Oh, yeah. You drive like an old man."

"Hey! I resemble that remark."

Katie looked at Joe. "Very funny, Curly."

"I'm impressed," Joe said. "You know The Three Stooges."

"My dad was a big fan. I remember watching it with him sometimes when I was little."

Joe smiled. "I knew there was a reason I liked your dad."

"You sure do know a lot about movies and TV shows for someone without a television."

"We bought our first television in the fifties, and I had always had one until about twenty years ago. It was some time after Marie died that I decided I was wasting my time sitting home in front of the tube, so around the same time I gave my car away, I also got rid of the television. It's amazing how much free time you have when you have no television. I started going outside and taking photographs again."

"Considering I made a living from television, I'm surprised that I agree we are better off without it."

Joe put his hand on Katie's knee. "You are smarter than I was at twice your age."

Katie took Joe's hand and said, "I was lucky to find a good mentor."

"Where are we going, by the way?"

"I think we should go on a date," Katie said. "There's an old movie theater near where I used to live that shows classic movies. I think you would like it."

"Do you know what's showing there?"

"No, and I don't care. Let's watch whatever it is."

"Sounds good to me," Joe said.

They drove to Milwaukee and parked near a theater that Joe guessed was around seventy years old. Its mid-century modern style, with neon lights and sleek curves, brought back memories of a simpler time. The marquee above the entrance read in bold, black letters: *Some Like It Hot*.

"I don't believe it," Joe said as they approached the main entrance. "I saw this movie years ago in a very similar theater."

"I take it you like my idea."

"Of course. You always have good ideas."

Their timing was perfect. The four o'clock show was about to start soon. Inside, the smell of fresh popcorn permeated the air. They found a seat near the back, and Joe went to the lobby to get popcorn while Katie saved his seat. He returned with a large bucket of popcorn and two bottles of water."

When the movie started, a feeling of nostalgia swept over Joe. He looked at Katie, who had her eyes glued to the screen while eating popcorn. He was happy he could share an old memory with her.

When the movie ended, and they stepped out into the crisp evening air, Katie asked, "Did you enjoy the movie?"

"I thought it was great. It had been so long since I had seen that film that I had forgotten almost everything. It was like seeing it for the first time."

"I never saw it, so it was seeing it for the first time for me. I must admit, I like old movies more than I thought I would."

They reached the car, and Joe opened the door for Katie. "They call it the golden age of cinema for a reason," he said.

***

Katie was in the mood for pizza, so they stopped at a nearby pizzeria. The last time they were there, they picked up a pizza and happened to see their main suspect drive by, so they followed the car and ate pizza during their impromptu stakeout. This time, they ate inside the restaurant.

After dinner, they returned to their hotel. Katie got her laptop and sat on the bed.

"What are you doing?" Joe asked.

"I think it's time to get back to work. I want to see what I can find about Scott Wilson."

"Do you think you can dig up anything useful?"

"I don't know, but we can't just do nothing."

Joe sat next to her and watched her work. She first went to Facebook and found Scott's profile. She scrolled through his posts for several minutes until Joe asked. "Do you see anything interesting?"

"Not really. He doesn't post much. When he does, it's usually photos of him with Sonia or other friends. Most of the photos involve drinking."

"So, no posts about him complaining about his job or anything like that?"

"No, nothing like that. In fact, the few work-related posts I see seem more like boasting. Like he's proud of what he's doing there."

"That doesn't sound like a man wanting to kill his boss."

"No, but some people are smart enough to keep their negativity off social media."

"What kind of stuff do you post, Katie?"

"I don't use Facebook too much anymore, but sometimes I post photos of you and me."

"Are you sure that's a good idea?" Joe asked. "I worry that twenty or thirty years from now, anyone in the world will be able to see those photos and compare how we look thirty years apart."

"Oh, no! I hadn't considered that. What do you think I should do?"

"I don't want to discourage you from doing what you like, but maybe you can stop posting personal photos."

"That's probably a good idea. I can also remove the ones I already posted."

Katie continued to look up records for Scott Wilson. After a few minutes, she said, "I don't see anything useful on the internet."

"Well, my dear, we'll just have to do things the old-fashioned way."

"What way is that?"

"Ask Sonia if she knows Max Allen's home address. I think we should pay him a visit tomorrow."

"I like the way you think," Katie said.

She texted Sonia the request and waited for a reply. A minute later, her phone beeped. She checked the message. It said, "I know his address, but why do you need it? Do you have a lead? Is it Max?"

Katie replied, "No. We don't have a lead, and we don't suspect Max. We have a question that needs clearing up."

"Ok," Sonia texted back. "Just a sec."

A minute later, Katie received a text with Max's address. She showed it to Joe, who said, "Okay, good. Now we have something we can do tomorrow."

Chapter 11

The following morning, Katie and Joe headed to see Max Allen. He lived in a modest home not far from the airport. They pulled into his driveway and parked next to a newer model red Ford Mustang. The Mustang was parked in front of an attached two-car garage. The house had one of those camera doorbells. Katie pushed the button, and they waited. After thirty seconds, the door opened, and Max stood there with a surprised look. "Good morning. I didn't expect to see you today. Forgive me, but I'm not great at remembering names."

"I'm Katie, and this is Joe."

"Oh, of course. What can I do for you, Katie and Joe?"

"That's a beautiful Mustang you have," Joe said.

"Thanks. I love Mustangs. I have a seventy-one in the garage that I'm restoring."

"Really? I'd like to see that," Joe said.

"Okay, sure. Let me put my shoes on. I'll be right out."

When he closed the door, Katie looked at Joe and said, "Really? We didn't come here to look at cars."

"Relax. He will be more willing to open up to us if we share a common interest. Besides, I really am interested."

The garage door opened a moment later, revealing an old, light blue Mustang. The paint was faded and had a few areas of rust, but the car was in relatively good condition for its age. The hood was off the car and leaning against the wall to the right. The engine was outside the car on a stand on the other side. Max stepped out of the garage, looked at Joe, and asked, "What do you think?"

"A Mach One. You have potential there. Is that the 429?"

"Sounds like you know your Mustangs."

"I looked into getting a sixty-eight, but my wife didn't like the idea. I had a Corvette a few years earlier, and she thought I should grow up."

Max looked at Katie and said, "Forcing a man to give up his toys might not be the best idea."

Katie, surprised at the criticism, said, "Wait a minute. He's not talking about me."

"Oh. I'm sorry. I thought you two were married."

"We are married," Katie said. "He's talking about his first wife, who died before we met."

Max looked at Joe and said, "Oh, I'm so sorry. That sucks. You're way too young to lose a wife."

"Thank you," Joe said. "We actually came here to talk about something other than cars."

"Okay, sure. What can I help you with?"

"We want to talk about the evening before Steve North died," Katie said.

"What do you want to know?"

"We learned someone entered the hangar at quarter to eight that evening. Do you know who that might have been?" Katie asked.

"No. I have no idea. Maybe Steve went to check on the aircraft."

"Katie looked at Joe, who said, "That's something we didn't consider."

"What time did you get off work that evening?"

"It was a little before six-thirty. I remember Steve coming back and telling us he appreciated all our hard work. He then told us to go home and rest. I thought it was strange. Do you think he knew he was going to die?"

"I doubt it," Joe said. "He knew the company was teetering on the edge and probably figured overworking his employees would not make much of a difference."

Max's eyes widened in surprise. "Teetering on the edge? What do you mean? Are you saying the company's in trouble?"

Joe looked at Katie, who said, "We're sorry to surprise you with this news, but that's why Steve North was flying to Minneapolis. He hoped to win over a big client by proving his plane could make the long trip. That is also why we are here. The perception that your aircraft might have a design defect could ruin the company. We need to prove someone sabotaged the plane as quickly as possible before Zero North runs out of money and is forced into bankruptcy."

Max gazed into the distance and slowly nodded. "That must be why they are moving the prototype to the hangar today."

"Today?" Katie asked, surprised. "It's Saturday."

"It was ready on Friday, but today was the earliest they could get a truck out here to pick it up." He looked at his watch. "I have to leave soon to help out."

"Why do they need engineers to load a plane on a truck?" Joe asked.

"They don't. It's probably being loaded on a truck as we speak. They need us to assemble it and prepare it for its first flight after it arrives at the hangar."

"Are they planning to fly it today?" Joe asked.

"That was the plan as far as I know."

"How long will it take until it's ready?" Katie asked. "We'd like to be there for the flight."

Max looked at his watch again. "If there are no delays in loading the aircraft, it should be at the hangar around ten. It will take about forty minutes to attach the wings and another hour, maybe two, to ensure everything is working properly. So, I would guess we could be flying as early as noon, but probably closer to one."

"We have a couple more questions," Joe said. "Where were you at a quarter to eight Monday night?"

"Really? Do you think I did this?"

"No," Katie said. "We don't know who did this yet. We just want to eliminate you so we can focus our attention on more likely candidates."

"Who is a more likely candidate?"

Katie looked at Joe and back at Max. "We don't want to start any rumors without more evidence."

"Okay. To answer your question, I came straight home after work and didn't leave the house until the next morning."

"Can you prove that?" Joe asked.

"Yes. My security system records movement. It would have a video of me coming home and no video of me leaving again. It will also show my car in the driveway."

"Can we see the videos?" Joe asked.

"No. We get so little privacy these days. I want to hang on to what little is left. I'll tell you what. If you suspect me, bring your evidence to the police. If they show up with a court order, I will be happy to show them the videos."

Joe looked at Katie and smiled. He looked back at Max and said. "One more question. Did everyone leave that evening at the same time as you?"

"Yes, I think so. I didn't do a head count, but I know all of us engineers left at the same time."

"Thanks so much for your time, Max," Katie said. "We'll see you at the hangar later."

When they got back in Katie's car, she asked, "Why did you smile at me back there?"

"I just found Max to be refreshing."

"Refreshing? Because he withheld evidence from us?"

"The world has changed, Katie. It used to be easy to keep to yourself. Now, everyone knows everyone else's business. I feel good whenever I see someone pushing back against that."

"I guess I understand, but it doesn't help us."

"I would rather see some crooks go free than have the world under surveillance."

After a pause, Katie nodded and said, "Yeah. I can't argue with you there."

"Do you want to go to the airport and watch them assemble their airplane?" Joe asked.

"Sure, but we have some time to kill. Let's find a gas station and fill my car up."

They found a gas station five minutes away. Joe filled the tank while Katie used their washroom. When she returned, she started the engine and said, "Oooh!"

Joe looked at her and asked, "Did the baby kick again?"

"Yes," Katie said, taking Joe's hand and placing it on her stomach. "Can you feel him?"

Joe smiled. "I can. He's an active little fellow."

"I think he's almost ready to come out."

"Maybe. We'll see."

"Can we feel him again? Since he's awake, I want him to know we are here."

"I'm sure he knows that, Katie."

"Maybe, but I want to be sure."

"You know, we can just talk to him. He has ears. He can hear."

"Really, Joe? Do you think he wants to hear when he can feel?"

Joe sighed, "Okay, fine, but not here. Pull around to the side."

Katie drove around to the side of the building and parked the car. Joe held her hand and connected to her. She loved the feeling of being connected to Joe and little Joey simultaneously. It was as if all three of them were one person. After a while, Joe let go and said, "I think he is happy."

"I think so, too. I'm ready to solve this case, have this baby, and go home."

"In that order?"

"Honestly, I'd like to have the baby now, but I don't want to fail Sonia."

"All we can do is try our best. If the baby comes first, that won't make us failures. Sonia knows that."

"I know, but think of all the people who could lose their jobs."

"Let's not think about that now. Let's head to the airport."

Chapter 12

When they reached Zero North's hangar, Katie parked behind the building, and they walked around to the front. They saw a semi-truck with three men and two women manually guiding the prototype aircraft down a ramp. By the time they walked to it, the aircraft was on the ground, and Max, Larry, and Scott were helping the truck driver remove the wings from the truck.

Sonia and Elena turned toward Katie and Joe. Sonia said, "Good morning, Katie. Good Morning, Joe. I didn't expect to see you here today."

"We thought it would be interesting to see how you transported and assembled your airplane," Katie said.

"Assembling it is no big deal. The cool part is watching it fly," Sonia said.

"Will you fly it today?" Joe asked.

"That's the plan. Except I won't be flying in it. Larry will be our test pilot."

After the truck pulled away and they moved the aircraft into the hangar, everyone except Sonia worked on installing the wings. They had it fully assembled in less than an hour. The three engineers tested all the components while Larry joined Sonia, Katie, and Joe."

"What do you think?" Larry asked.

"I'm impressed," Joe said. "I expected you to need a forklift to get the plane out of the truck."

"No. It's small and light enough to roll it on and off. Of course, we secure it well so it can't move around inside."

"Are you worried about flying it?" Katie asked. "I mean, it's the first time it has flown. Is it dangerous?"

"I'm a bit of a history buff," Larry said. "I look at history to put things into perspective. Do you know anything about the WASP program during World War II?"

"No. What's WASP?" Katie asked.

"It stands for Women Airforce Service Pilots," Joe said.

"That's right," Larry said. "I see you know your history."

"Joe is an expert on the twentieth century," Katie said. "It's the twenty-first century that he knows nothing about."

Larry laughed. "At his age? That's hard to believe. All you Gen Zs know everything about technology."

"Joe is the exception," Katie said.

"I like a simple life," Joe said. "Is there anything wrong with that?"

"Nothing at all," Larry said. "I respect you for that. Anyway, the WASPs flew new aircraft from the factories to airbases, mostly within the United States. From there, many were shipped or flown to Europe. They freed male pilots for service in the war. Thirty-eight women lost their lives flying over three hundred and fifty thousand missions. That's a little more than one out of every ten thousand flights. Many, if not most, of those flights were brand new aircraft right off the factory floor, and that was eighty years ago or more. Compared to that, I think I have very little to worry about."

"I guess if you look at it that way, it seems pretty safe," Katie said.

They moved inside, sat on the sofa and chairs, and talked until Scott announced that the aircraft was ready to fly. Larry stood up and said, "Wish me luck."

Everyone wished him luck and watched as he got into the aircraft. He taxied to the runway, and after a short pause, they watched the small plane take off into a steep climb. Everyone clapped and cheered. Larry took several wide loops around the airport and landed fifteen minutes later. When he arrived back at the hangar, everyone congratulated him and shook his hand.

"That was great," Katie said. "We are so happy everything went well."

"Thank you. It feels like a great weight has been lifted. Now, we need to work on bringing in some money."

"Joe and I haven't had lunch yet, so we'll say goodbye for now," Katie said.

"I planned on taking everyone out for pizza if you want to come along," Larry said.

Katie looked at Joe, who nodded. "Sure. That sounds great," she said.

They followed everyone to an Italian restaurant about five minutes away. The staff seated them at two tables that they had pushed together. After discussing their options, Larry ordered three pizzas and two pitchers of beer. Katie asked for an unsweetened iced tea.

When the beer arrived, Scott poured some of it into Sonia's glass. Katie poked Joe, who whispered, "I think we need to tell her."

Katie said, "Sonia. I just remembered there's something in the car I need to show you. Can you come outside for a minute?"

"Sure," she said, getting out of her seat and following Katie outside.

Joe said, "Excuse me," before getting up and joining them.

When they got to the car, Katie zipped up her coat and put her hands in her pockets. "We actually have something important to tell you, and we didn't want anyone else to hear it." She looked at Joe.

"Uh, I don't know how to say this without sounding crazy or creepy, but you're pregnant," Joe said.

Sonia's eyes widened, and her mouth hung open. She looked at Katie, who nodded. "Is this some kind of joke? Why would you tell me that?"

"It's not a joke," Katie said. "We didn't want you to drink alcohol."

"Even if I were pregnant, which I'm not, how would you even know that?"

"Joe has a special gift. He felt the baby when he pulled you from the wreckage."

She looked at Joe. "What special gift do you have? Are you telling me you are some kind of psychic?"

"I wouldn't use that word," Joe said, "but I am able to feel things that other people can't."

She shook her head. "I don't believe it. There's no such thing as psychics. It's all a bunch of hooey."

"I'm not claiming to be a psychic," Joe said. "It's different than that. You don't have to believe us. We are just asking that you avoid alcohol until you know for sure."

Sonia was quiet for a moment before saying, "When you were at my house and said you were a recovering alcoholic, was that true?"

Joe shook his head. "No. I'm sorry. I hate lying, but the truth would not have gone over well that night."

"I suppose not. Okay, fine. I won't drink tonight, but I will be very disappointed in your investigative abilities if you are wrong."

"That's fair," Katie said. "We didn't want to tell you this way, but felt we had no choice."

When they returned to their table, Scott asked, "What was that all about?"

"Nothing important. Just business stuff," Sonia said.

They stayed for another hour. It felt like a celebration. Everyone was in a good mood except Sonia, who seemed troubled.

After leaving the restaurant, Katie and Joe returned to their hotel room. They sat on the bed together, and Katie held Joe's hand. "I'm so happy I have a supportive husband. I can't imagine being afraid to tell you I'm pregnant."

"Having a child is a great responsibility. It can be a source of stress for many people."

"Yeah, I get that. Sonia must realize her relationship is on the rocks. I'm sure that doesn't help."

"No, it doesn't. She's probably having a lot of mixed emotions right now, or she will be after she does a pregnancy test."

"I'm not looking forward to that conversation," Katie said.

Ten minutes later, Katie's phone rang. She looked at the number and said, "This is it." She pushed the answer button. "Hi, Sonia."

"How did you know? Tell me the truth," Sonia said in a loud whisper.

"I told you Joe has a gift."

After a long pause, she said, "I don't know how it's possible, but Joe was right. I'm pregnant."

"Congratulations. We are both happy for you. What did Scott say?"

"I haven't told him yet."

"I think he deserves to know," Katie said.

"Yes, he does, but now is not a good time. We discussed having children, but he thought we should wait until after the company became profitable. What if we both find ourselves unemployed?"

"That won't change the fact that you are pregnant now."

"No. I suppose it won't."

"Were you on birth control?" Katie asked.

"I was, but I stopped taking it. It was causing nausea and headaches. Our sex life was almost non-existent anyway. Scott was always too tired. I figured it wouldn't matter if I stopped."

"It seems 'almost' is the keyword here."

"It must have happened over the Christmas break."

"You're going to have to tell him sooner or later," Katie said. "Sooner would be better."

"Larry and I are flying to Minneapolis tomorrow. I will feel more comfortable telling Scott if we can convince the customer to place an order."

"Are you sure that plane is ready for a long flight like that?" Katie asked. "Maybe Larry can fly it, and you can drive there."

"No. We need to show the customer we are confident in our product."

"That makes sense, but aren't you scared?" Katie asked. "You crashed just a few days ago. Are you sure you're ready to try again?"

"No. I'm not sure about anything, but I know how important this is, especially now. Besides, this aircraft has safety features that the other one didn't have, plus a slightly longer range. I'm sure we'll make it."

"You need to check that plane from top to bottom," Joe said. "I mean you, personally, and Larry. Don't trust your safety to other people."

"Do you think someone wanted to hurt the company and not Steve?"

"We don't know," Joe said. "If it were the company they were after, they'd be under much more scrutiny now, but I'd still be careful. Better safe than sorry."

"I'll contact Larry and make sure we get to the hangar before anyone else. We'll leave around nine if you want to see us off."

"If this baby doesn't decide to grace us with his presence, we will be there," Katie said.

***

A little while later, as they sat on the bed together, Joe said, "I've been thinking. We are getting nowhere on this case. I think we need to start from scratch."

"Okay," Katie said slowly. "What are you thinking about?"

"Let's go back to when we discovered someone had sabotaged the plane. What was the first thing we assumed?"

Katie paused and then said, "I guess we assumed someone wanted to kill Steve North or his company."

"What if neither of those is true?"

"If neither of those is true, what else could it be?"

"Well, there was more than one person in that airplane?"

Katie's eyes widened, and her mouth hung open. She was silent for several seconds and finally said, "Oh, wow! I hadn't considered that. Wait a minute.

Sonia said she talked Steve into taking her with him at the last minute. How could she be the target? She wasn't supposed to be on that airplane."

"That's why we didn't consider her a target before, but suppose the killer knew her well enough to know she would talk her way into going with Steve on that flight."

"Who would know her that well except for . . . Oh, my God! Scott."

"That's what I was thinking."

"Why would Scott want to kill Sonia? I mean, I know they have a less-than-perfect marriage, but that's no reason to kill someone. They could get a divorce."

"Do you remember Sonia saying their house was a wedding gift from her parents?"

"Yeah. What does that have to do with anything?"

"She told me her parents put only her name on the deed. In Wisconsin, do you know what would happen to that house in a divorce?"

"I'm not a lawyer, Joe. I have no idea. What are you getting at?"

"Since the house was a gift to Sonia and Sonia alone, she would retain all rights to it after the divorce. On the other hand, if she were to die in an accident, Scott would get the house."

"How do you know all this?"

"I've lived in Wisconsin since well before you were born, and as I said before, I do a lot of reading."

"I think you're onto something, Joe, but I'm not sure a house is a good enough reason to kill your wife."

"Did she have a life insurance policy?"

"Get me my laptop, and I'll look."

Joe brought Katie's laptop to her. She looked through the files that Billy had sent her, found the correct one, and opened it. After reading for several seconds, she said, "They each have a quarter-million-dollar life insurance policy."

"That, combined with the house, could be a good reason for murder," Joe said.

"I think we have our first real suspect. The question is, how do we prove it?"

"I have no idea. I'm not even certain I am right about this."

"Right now, it makes more sense than anything else. Maybe Billy can help."

"Billy? What can he do?"

"Billy's the best hacker I know. Well, he's the only hacker I know, but that's beside the point. Anyway, I bet he could hack into Scott's phone."

"How will that help us?"

"Remember Alan Hutchinson showing us his location history on his phone?"

"Oh, yes. That's brilliant. Do you think Billy can get that information?"

"I'm not certain, but I think there's a good chance, assuming Scott has that feature turned on," Katie said. "The only problem is that today is Saturday, and he is off until Monday."

"That is a problem," Joe said. "What about Eric? He's good with computers."

"Eric is taking classes for hotel management, not computer hacking."

"Let's call him and ask. Maybe he can do it or figure it out."

"Okay, but I don't know Scott's phone number."

"Can't you ask Sonia?"

"I can, but what if she wants to know why we want it?"

"Tell her you need backup numbers in case you have questions and can't contact her while she's away. Add other names to the list so Scott won't be the main focus."

"Good idea," Katie said, sending Sonia a text. In addition to Scott's number, she added Max, Larry, and Elena to the list.

A few minutes later, Sonia responded with numbers for all the names on the list.

Katie called Eric and put the phone on speaker. "Hi, Katie," he said.

"Hi, Eric. We have a question for you," Katie said. "We need someone to hack into someone's phone and retrieve their location history. Unfortunately, the person who usually helps us with tech stuff is off on the weekends. Could you do that, or do you know someone who could help?"

"Oh, wow! Do you have a suspect?"

"We don't know for sure, but it might be Scott," Joe said.

"Scott? You mean Sonia's husband?"

"That's him," Katie said.

"Well, I don't know how to get that information, but I have a friend from school who might be able to help. He's learning cybersecurity. Programming is like his primary language. I can't promise anything, but if he can do it, he will need as much information about the guy as possible. Minimally, he'll need his full name, address, and phone number. If you have his birthday, place of birth, email, and anything else that identifies him, that will help."

"I can do better than that," Katie said. "I have a full report on him that our tech friend, Billy, sent us."

"That will work even better," Eric said.

"Okay. Thanks so much, Eric. I will email it to you right away."

When Katie hung up, she found Billy's email and forwarded it to Eric.

Chapter 13

Katie and Joe arrived at the hangar around eight the following morning. They found Sonia inside the aircraft and Elena under it. They both seemed to be checking the plane for anomalies. Sonia saw them come in and stepped out of the plane. "Good morning, Katie. Good morning, Joe. How are you today?"

Upon hearing that, Elena stood up and greeted them, too.

"Where's Larry?" Joe asked.

"Larry called this morning and said he wasn't feeling well," Sonia said. "He thinks the pizza he had last night did him in. I called Elena and asked if she could fly me to Minneapolis. Fortunately, she was happy to do it."

"You're not concerned about flying a plane you've never flown before?" Katie asked.

"I flew the first prototype," Elena said. "It was very easy to fly, and this version is no different as far as the aeronautics are concerned."

"Have you finished checking the plane out?" Katie asked.

"Yes," Sonia said. "We just finished as you walked in. Everything is good to go."

"Did you open the panel behind the seat?" Joe asked.

"That was the first place I looked," Sonia said.

A few minutes later, Scott and Max arrived together. Scott walked up to Sonia, held her hands, and said, "Are you sure you want to fly again so soon after the accident?"

"It wasn't an accident," Sonia said. "You know that."

"I know. I meant to say 'crash.' Are you sure you are up to this?"

"I'll be fine, Scott. I'm a little nervous, but it's nothing I can't handle. It's nice that you are worried about me, though."

"Of course, I'm worried about you. You're my wife, and I love you."

Katie looked at Joe and almost imperceivably shook her head.

"Thank you, Scott. You don't tell me that enough."

"Well, I should. That is something I need to work on."

"Are you guys ready to get started?" Max asked.

"Yes, of course," Sonia said. "Let's get this plane in the air."

The three engineers got to work, ensuring everything on the aircraft was in proper working order. They hadn't checked it after Larry's flight the previous day and wanted to ensure nothing had changed. Once the aircraft was thoroughly tested and in production, the pre-flight routine could be streamlined and shortened to less than ten minutes. For now, especially considering the importance of the flight that morning, they wanted to ensure nothing would go wrong.

Katie's phone beeped, and she checked it. "It's a message from Eric."

"What does it say?"

Katie walked outside, and Joe followed her. "It's a timeline for Scott," she said. "They did it."

"That's great. Where was he that night?" Joe asked.

"It shows him leaving work at six twenty-five, driving for six minutes, and arriving at a house on Fox Ridge Drive, where he stayed until seven twenty-six. From there, he drove to a gas station and then straight home, arriving at seven fifty-three. Eric says the house belongs to Elena. So now we know he's a cheating bastard."

"Yes, he is, but that also proves he didn't plant that bomb."

"That leaves us back on square one again."

"We've been there before."

A few minutes later, Katie's phone rang. It was a local number, but she didn't recognize it. She answered, saying, "Hello."

"Hello. Is this Katie?" came a woman's voice on the other end.

"Yes, it is. Who's this?"

"This is Christine Bellamy from WB Aerial Photography. You left me a message saying it was important that you talk to me."

"Oh, yes. I didn't expect to hear from you until Monday."

"Yeah, well. When you have your own business, weekends are not always a luxury."

"We are at the airport now, but are in the middle of something. Can we meet you in half an hour or so?"

"I'll be here," Christine said.

Twenty minutes later, the engineers disconnected their equipment, and Scott gave Sonia a thumbs-up. He attached a pull bar to the aircraft and pulled it from the hangar. Elena and Sonia got in, waited for approval, then taxied to the runway and took off.

Katie and Joe watched until their plane was out of sight, and then Katie said, "Let's go see a woman about her security footage."

"Okay," Joe said, taking Katie's hand.

***

They walked at a casual pace behind Zero North's hangar to the hangar belonging to WB Aerial Photography. The large hangar door was open, revealing an old, high-wing World War II single-engine airplane painted olive drab. It looked in good condition, with the United States Army Air Forces symbol still painted on the side.

"Wow!" Joe said.

A woman, perhaps forty years old, wearing grey overalls and a baseball cap, was working on the engine. When she heard Joe, she turned, looked at Katie, and said, "Good morning. Are you Katie?"

"That's me," Katie said.

"That's a beautiful airplane," Joe said. "I haven't seen a Grasshopper in ages."

The woman picked up a towel and said, "Ages? I'm surprised you've ever seen one."

Katie stepped forward and said, "Hi. My name is Katie Novak, and this is my husband, Joe. He's a big World War II buff."

"I can see that," the woman said. "I'd shake your hand, but I don't want to get you dirty. My name's Christine Bellamy."

"It's nice to meet you, Christine," Joe said. "I'm curious where you got the plane."

"I bought it years ago from a guy who got old and couldn't fly it anymore. He bought it at a government auction a few years after the war. At least, that's what he told me. I'm surprised someone your age would be interested in World War II aircraft. Did you see it in a video game or something?"

"No. I haven't played a video game since Pong," Joe said.

Christine looked confused at the statement, and Katie changed the subject, saying, "We're actually here for a different reason. We are private investigators looking into the death of Steven North."

"Oh, yes. That's big news around here. I didn't know him well, but I was sad to hear what had happened. What is it that I can help you with?"

"We believe that the killer entered Zero North's hangar on the sixth at around seven forty-five in the evening," Joe said.

"Killer? What do you mean by 'killer?' I thought it was an accident."

"Someone planted an explosive device on his airplane," Katie said.

"Wow! I don't believe it. Nothing like that has ever happened around here before."

"We need your help," Joe said. "One of your cameras points toward Zero North's hangar. We need to see if it might have captured a car the night that I mentioned."

"Well, I guess you can look at the footage, but I doubt you can make anything out from that distance."

"It's worth a shot," Joe said.

"Okay, follow me."

She led them to a small office in the corner of the hangar. She sat down in front of a computer and brought up the security files. "You said it was the sixth?"

"Yes," Joe replied. "Around seven forty-five."

She found the appropriate file and opened it. The video was black and white, which was normal for videos shot at night. They could see Zero North's hangar in the distance. They watched for over a minute before they saw headlights. The vehicle stopped in front of Zero North's hangar and turned off the lights. They saw someone get out and head toward the door. After a few seconds, the person went inside. The distance was too far for any detail to be discernible. The person looked more like a blob. After five minutes, the blob returned, got in the vehicle, and did a U-turn before heading back the way it came. As it turned, Katie and Joe could see it was a small pickup truck.

"Can you pause it?" Joe asked.

Christine hit the pause button, and they studied the image.

"It's a pickup truck, but I can't tell what kind," Katie said.

Joe shook his head. "There's not much detail in the image."

"It's one of those mid-sized trucks like a Takoma or a Ranger," Christine said.

"Who drives a pickup truck?" Katie asked. "I don't think it's Scott."

"No. I remember when he picked Sonia up at the resort, he drove a sporty-looking car, like a Charger. Besides, we already established it wasn't him."

"Sonia doesn't have a pickup either," Katie said. "She drives an Explorer. Helen drove some kind of sedan when she came to the resort. Maybe Steve North drove a truck, and he came to check on the plane that night."

"I don't know, but we need to figure out who drives a pickup truck," Joe said. "I have a feeling we need to do it quickly."

"I think you're right."

Katie took out her phone and dialed a number. When it was answered, she said, "Eric! We need information fast. Is your friend still available?"

"He's here with me. What do you need?"

"Scott is probably not the killer. We need to know who drives a pickup truck. The possible names are in the files I sent you. Start with Alan Hutchinson, Arthur King, Larry Cooper, Elena Petrova, and Steven North. Call me as soon as you find out. Let your friend know we will pay him for his time."

"Okay, but I think finding a killer is payment enough."

When Katie hung up, she turned to Christine and said, "Thank you so much. That was a great help." She asked for a pen and paper and wrote her email address on it. "Can you please send a copy of that to me?"

By the time they returned to the car, Katie was breathing hard.

"Are you okay?" Joe asked.

Katie put her hand on her heart and said, "I think the excitement is getting to me."

Joe took Katie's hand and connected to her. He could feel she was having a mild panic attack. He could also feel her hormones were out of balance, probably caused by her pregnancy. He felt she was getting too much of one hormone and not enough of another. Joe didn't know each hormone by name. He just learned how to manipulate them to get the outcome he wanted. After a couple of minutes, Katie's heart slowed, and her breathing returned to normal.

"Maybe this is getting to be too much for you right now," Joe said.

"I'm fine now, thanks to you."

"You're fine now, but I worry about the next time."

"If you're thinking about quitting, forget it." Katie put her thumb and index finger close together. "We are this close to finding the killer."

Just then, Katie's phone rang. She answered it, and Eric's voice came through her car's speakers. "We checked those names, and only one has a pickup truck: Elena Petrova. She has a white 2018 Ford Ranger."

"Katie looked at Joe, "Oh, my God!"

"That's what I was afraid of," Joe said.

"We have to go, Eric," Katie said. "Thanks for your help."

When Katie hung up, she immediately dialed Sonia's number. It rang four times and then went to voicemail. Katie left a message. "Sonia, this is Katie. Elena is the one who planted the bomb. She wasn't after Steve. She was after you. If you get this message, get away immediately and call the police."

Katie hung up the phone and looked at Joe. "She's in trouble. Her phone rang, so she was in the range of a cell tower, but she didn't pick up."

"Call 911," Joe said.

Katie called 911, told the dispatcher the story in a nutshell, and asked her to contact the Minneapolis police department."

Joe opened his door and got out of the car. "We need to go back and talk to Christine again."

Katie got out and hurried to catch up to Joe. When they returned to the hangar, Christine was again working on her engine. She turned and said, "Did you forget something?"

"We need your help," Joe said. "We just learned who the killer is. Steve North was not her target. She's flying to Minneapolis with her intended victim as we speak. We think she plans to kill her. Can you fly us there? We'll pay whatever it takes."

"I'm sorry. I'd do it for free to save a life, but I have a broken control cable. I ordered a replacement, but it won't arrive until tomorrow."

"Thanks anyway," Joe said. He grabbed Katie's hand and almost pulled her out of the hangar.

"Slow down, Joe. I can't move that fast."

"I'm sorry, but we need to catch Scott before he leaves."

"Scott? How do you know he and Elena aren't working together?"

"I don't know, but if he's not part of this, he might be able to help."

"You go ahead. I'll catch up."

Joe ran as fast as he could back to Zero North's hangar. When he reached the front, he saw Scott and Max standing outside. He arrived just in time as the large door was closing. Joe took a deep breath and almost yelled, "Scott! I need to talk to you. It's important."

Scott looked at Max and said, "It's okay. I'll see you tomorrow."

Max walked away, and Joe walked toward the side of the hangar, motioning for Scott to follow, just as Katie arrived.

"What's this all about?" Scott asked.

"Listen! Sonia's in trouble, and we don't have time for lies. We know you are having an affair with Elena, and we know she was the one who planted the bomb in Steve's airplane. We need to know if you were part of it. We will find out one way or another, so tell us now."

"Wait! What? How do you know Elena did that? What proof do you have?"

"What kind of man cheats on his pregnant wife?" Katie asked.

"Pregnant? Slow down. What the hell is going on here?"

Joe looked at Katie, who said, "Elena planted that bomb not to kill Steve North but to kill your wife."

Scott stepped back and shook his head. "That's crazy. Elena wouldn't do that. She's not a killer."

"Are you sure about that?" Katie asked.

"Look. I admit it. We had an affair, but I went to her house to call it off that night."

"You were there for almost an hour. That's a lot of calling off," Katie said.

Scott's eyes widened. "How in the world would you know that?"

"It's what we do," Joe said.

"Look, Elena didn't take kindly to me breaking up with her. She threatened to tell Sonia. It took a lot of convincing to keep her from doing that."

"Then, after you left her house, she drove straight to the hangar and planted an explosive in the back of Steve's airplane," Katie said.

"That's crazy. How would she even know Sonia would be on that flight?"

"How did you know Steve planned to fly to Minneapolis the next morning?" Joe asked.

"Elena told me." Suddenly, a look of shock came over Scott's face. "Oh, my God. She knew I would tell Sonia, and she knew Sonia would want to go with him."

"Now they are flying to Minneapolis alone together. What do you think will happen?" Katie asked.

Scott put his hands on his head. "Oh, Jeez. What did I do?"

"We need to get to Minneapolis as soon as possible," Joe said. "You said you were taking lessons. How far along were you? Could you fly us there?"

"No. I'm not licensed. Even if I had a license, I don't have a plane."

"What about Larry? Does he have a plane here?" Katie asked.

"Yeah, he does, but he's sick, and I couldn't fly it."

"If you're worried about losing a license you don't have, I think your wife's life is more important."

"That's not why I can't fly it. I never learned how to navigate. I would be lost ten miles from the airport."

"That's a problem," Joe said.

"We need to go see Larry," Katie said. She turned to Scott. "Can you get Larry's plane ready to fly?"

"Sure. If Larry is up to flying, it will be ready when you return."

***

Twenty minutes after Elena and Sonia left the airport, Sonia's phone rang. She dug it out of her purse and saw that Katie was calling. "Don't answer that," she heard Elena say. She looked to her left and saw Elena pointing a gun at her.

Sonia's eyes widened, and her face turned pale. Her eyes darted between Elena's face and the gun pointed at her head. Her mouth hung open as if trying to speak, but no words came out. Finally, she said, "What the hell? What are you doing?"

"Shut up and give me the phone."

Sonia slowly handed her phone to Elena, who tossed it behind the seats. It rang one more time before stopping.

"Why are you pointing a gun at me? Are you crazy? What is going on?"

Elena glanced out her window and quickly returned her attention to Sonia. "I want you to shut up and look the other way. If I catch you looking this way, I will shoot you."

Sonia looked out her window, but she didn't shut up. "If you shoot me, you'll have a hard time cleaning up the evidence."

"I brought along some bleach cleaner just in case. Now, shut up."

Elena continued to look out her window. She needed to find the landing area she was looking for. When she spotted it, she started to descend.

Sonia noticed they were descending. After a minute, the plane skimmed above a field of barren farmland. "You're landing? There's no airport here."

"Elena said nothing. She continued to descend, bringing them down onto a lonely road in the middle of nowhere. The aircraft bounced once and then quickly slowed. Just before it stopped, it encountered a patch of ice and veered off the road into a ditch.

Sonia looked around. On one side of the road was farmland covered in snow for as far as the eye could see. There wasn't a farmhouse in sight. On the other side stood a large grouping of trees, perhaps an entire forest. Sonia wasn't sure. "Are you going to tell me what's going on now?"

**

Scott gave Larry's address to Katie, and she and Joe raced to his house. He lived only five minutes away from the airport. Katie rang the doorbell and waited. After thirty seconds, Larry's wife answered the door. "Can I help you?" she asked.

"Hi. I'm Katie, and this is Joe. We have an emergency and need to speak with Larry right away."

Larry's voice came from inside the house, "It's okay, Alice. Let them in."

They found Larry in the living room on a reclining chair. He had his head back and his feet up. A blanket covered his body. "Sonia's in danger," Katie said. "Elena set the bomb on Steve's plane."

A shocked look came over Larry's face. "Elena? Are you sure?"

"Yes, we're sure," Katie said. "Steve wasn't her target. She wanted to kill Sonia."

Alice, who was behind them listening in, said, "Oh, my! That's terrible."

"It's worse than you know, Honey," Larry said. "The two of them are flying together as we speak."

"Why would Elena want to kill Sonia?" Larry's wife asked.

"Jealousy," Joe said.

"We need you to fly us to Minneapolis," Katie said to Larry.

"Me? No. I need to be within twenty feet of a bathroom. I'm sorry."

"If I can make you better, will you fly us there?" Joe asked.

"If you can make me better, I'd fly you anywhere you want to go, but how could you do that?"

Katie touched Joe's arm and asked, "Are you sure?"

"We need to trust him," Joe said.

"Trust me? With what?" Larry asked.

"I need your word that anything you see here today will stay between us," Joe said.

Larry hesitated. "Sure, but what are we talking about?"

"Give me your hand," Joe said.

Larry reluctantly extended his hand, and Joe held it. He connected to him and could feel what was wrong. Even though he kept Larry from feeling what he felt, he didn't bother trying to hide that he was a healer.

After several seconds, Joe said, "It feels like someone gave you high doses of a potent laxative."

"How could you know that?"

"Joe has a special gift," Katie said.

After several seconds, Larry said, "If that's true, it must have happened at that pizza restaurant. The symptoms started soon after I got home."

"Elena must have spiked your drink," Katie said.

Larry shook his head. "That snake. I thought my beer tasted a little weird."

Joe worked on healing Larry. He directed his intestinal muscles to relax. That helped with part of the problem, but he was also dehydrated. He directed his cells to reabsorb some of the water that was lost.

"We need a glass of water," Joe said.

Alice rushed into the kitchen and came back with a glass of water. She handed it to Joe, who gave it to Larry. "Drink this," Joe said.

Larry drank the water while Joe continued instructing Larry's cells to absorb water. He knew the cells wouldn't absorb the water in his stomach, but he also knew the water would help him later. Joe let go of Larry's hand and said, "Okay, you should be good now."

Larry stood up and stayed still for several seconds. He put his hand on his stomach and pushed. I don't believe it. I feel fine."

Alice said, "Are you sure, Honey? Did it really work?"

"Yes. I think it worked. I feel great." He looked at Joe and said, "You need to tell me how you did that."

"Later," Joe said. "Right now, we need to save Sonia."

Larry followed Katie and Joe to the airport in his car. When they arrived, Scott had the airplane ready and fully fueled. It was a four-seat Cessna. It had high wings, unlike Zero North's prototype. It was also bigger than the prototype.

"How fast will this fly?" Katie asked.

"It's a bit faster than our prototype, but we have no chance of catching up with them if that's what you're getting at."

"I know," Katie said. "I just want to hurry."

They all got in the aircraft. Katie sat in the back with Joe, and Scott sat up front with Larry. Once they were in the air, Scott took out his phone and said, "I think I can locate Sonia's phone."

"How can you do that?" Joe asked.

"I know her login information. If I can log into her account, I should be able to locate her phone. That will give me her GPS coordinates."

"If you can do that, that would be great," Katie said.

After a couple of minutes, Scott said, "I've got it. Her phone is offline or out of range, but I have her last known position." He held the phone up, showed Larry the map, and then showed it to Katie and Joe. That's not too far from the resort," Joe said. "Did they crash?"

"I hope not," Larry said. "It could just be that her phone lost contact with cell towers, but it is concerning because they wouldn't be flying that high. She should have picked up another tower by now."

"We need to check it out," Scott said. "Can you fly over that location?"

Larry looked at Scott and said, "Give me the GPS coordinates."

Scott called out the numbers, and Larry entered them into his navigational computer. After a few seconds, he said, "It's on the way. We'll be there in twelve minutes."

Chapter 14

"Get out!" Elena commanded.

Sonia hesitated. Her pulse pounded. Did she want her out so she could shoot her without making a mess inside the aircraft? She didn't know, but she wasn't going to make it easy for her.

"Get out!" Elena repeated, pressing the gun hard against her head.

Sonia slowly exited the airplane. She wanted to resist but hoped cooperating would keep her alive long enough to think of a way out of this mess. Elena got out on her side and quickly met up with Sonia on the other side. "Throw your coat into the plane," Elena said.

"Are you kidding? It's twenty-five degrees out here. I'll freeze to death."

"Put your coat in the plane. I won't say it again.

Sonia slowly removed her coat and tossed it into the airplane.

"Now, move away."

Sonia slowly did what she was told. "Why are you doing this?" she asked, tears streaming down her face.

"If you want to live, plead for your life."

Sonia's eyes narrowed. She said nothing for several seconds. Finally, after seeing no alternative, she said, "Please, Elena, have a heart. Please don't shoot me. I was always nice to you. You have no reason to want to kill me."

"Pathetic," Elena said. "I can't imagine why he would choose you over me."

A hint of bewilderment showed on Sonia's face. "What? Who are you talking about? Scott? Have you been sleeping with my husband?"

"Ding, ding, ding. You get a prize. I'm going to let you walk out of here."

Elena pointed her gun at Sonia and fired. A sharp pain ripped through her thigh, and she cried out before falling to the ground. The bullet hit the outside part of Sonia's right thigh. Blood oozed from her leg. She put her hand over the entry point while she continued to cry in pain.

"Get up!" Elena demanded.

Sonia looked up at Elena pleadingly. "My God, Elena. Stop this. Do you want to spend the rest of your life in prison?"

"Prison? You attacked me. You learned Scott was cheating on you with me, so you forced me to land here and then tried to shoot me. Unfortunately for you, I managed to get the gun away from you and shoot you in the leg. You then took advantage of my desire not to kill you and scrambled into the woods, where you succumbed to the elements and loss of blood."

"You're crazy. Nobody will believe that."

"Sure, they will. You used Scott's gun that he kept in his glove compartment, where a jealous wife would have easy access to it?"

Sonia's mouth hung open with the realization that she was going to die out there, and Elena could possibly get away with it. Still, she held out hope that justice would prevail. Her biggest regret was that her baby would die with her. "My investigators will see right through that," she said.

"Oh, please. They don't have a clue. Now, get up and move."

Sonia stayed where she was. Elena fired another shot, which hit the ground near Sonia's feet. She struggled to stand up, wincing in pain. Elena fired another shot at Sonia's feet, causing her to pick up the pace. She made it to the tree line and soon disappeared out of sight.

Elena returned to the airplane, found her phone, and dialed 911. She figured it would take a long time before an ambulance got to her, and Sonia would be dead by then. Nothing happened. She looked at her phone and saw she had no signal. "Shit!" she said out loud.

She got out of the aircraft and thought. If she could get the plane back up in the air, she could call from there. Unfortunately, it was nose-first in a ditch. She grabbed hold of the tail wing and pulled. The plane moved slightly but then rolled forward again. She moved to the front and tried to push it out of the ditch. After several unsuccessful attempts, she gave up. Her only hope was that a motorist would drive by, which seemed unlikely anytime soon.

After several minutes, she started feeling cold, got inside the aircraft, and closed the door. She then saw an airplane fly overhead.

***

"We're approaching the coordinates," Larry announced.

Everyone looked out their window for the aircraft. Scott saw it first. "There it is! Ahead at one o'clock."

Larry dove slightly to get a better look. "It looks like it's still intact," he said. "She put it down on that road."

"Call it in," Joe said.

Larry got on the radio, said there was an aircraft down, and gave the GPS location. He also said it was a possible kidnapping and they should send the police as well as an ambulance.

"You need to land," Katie said.

"I can't land there. It's not a runway. It's too narrow."

"Elena did it," Katie said.

"Please, Larry," Scott said. "My wife's life is in danger."

Larry shook his head and said, "I can't believe I'm doing this."

He circled around and descended toward the road. It was a bumpy landing, but he kept the aircraft on the road. He brought the plane to a near standstill but kept it moving forward slowly until they arrived near the prototype aircraft. Elena emerged from the plane, waving her arms at them.

Everyone got out, and Elena said, "I'm so glad you found me. Sonia went crazy. She tried to kill me."

Scott looked at her with disdain. "What did you do, Elena?"

"Me? Are you seriously accusing me? Scott, you know me."

Joe pointed at the ground, "Look. There's blood, and it leads into the woods."

Scott looked back at Elena, who said, "I told you she tried to kill me. I fought back, and she fled into the woods."

Scott pointed at Elena and said, "You stay here. You've done enough already." He then walked quickly towards the woods, followed by Larry.

Joe turned to Katie and said, "You should wait here."

"You want me to wait with her?"

Joe looked at Elena and said, "Good point."

Katie took Joe's hand, and they followed Scott and Larry into the woods. Scott found Sonia about twenty yards from the tree line. She was lying on the ground, unconscious. He quickly took off his coat and covered her.

"She's lost a lot of blood. We need to get her out of here now."

"No!" Joe yelled. "Don't move her yet."

"She's gonna die if we don't get her out of here soon," Scott said.

Joe knelt next to Sonia and held her hand. "We need to stop the bleeding first."

"How are you going to do that?" Scott asked.

Joe held up his hand as if asking for silence. He connected to Sonia and immediately went to work, clotting the blood where the bullet entered her thigh. He then instructed her body to push the bullet the rest of the way out and clotted the blood at the exit. Once the bleeding stopped, he instructed the muscles in her extremities to shiver. It was the only thing he could do at the time to slow down the onset of frostbite. He let go of her hand and said, "Okay, we can move her now."

As Scott and Larry picked up Sonia, "Katie said, "Uh, Joe, we have another problem."

Joe turned to her and froze at the look of shock on her face. She said, "My water just broke."

His heart skipped a beat as he raced to her side. "What else can go wrong today?"

"Stop where you are," came Elena's voice.

Everyone turned and saw her holding a gun. She pointed it at Scott and Larry. "Put her down!" she demanded.

Scott and Larry gently set Sonia on the ground. Her eyes flickered open, but no one noticed. Scott then stepped between Elena and Sonia. "Put the gun down, Elena."

"No!" she cried, tears forming in her eyes. "It was supposed to be you and me. It still can be."

"No, it can't," Scott said, stepping forward.

"You never really loved me, did you? You just used me like every other man. You're all the same."

Scott stepped forward again.

"Stay where you are. Don't move."

"Please, Elena. Give me the gun," Scott said, holding out his hand and taking another step forward.

Elena fired. The bullet struck Scott dead center, just below the rib cage. Scott winced in pain and fell over. Joe, seeing an opportunity, tackled Elena. She hit the ground hard with Joe on top of her. The impact caused her to drop the gun, which Larry quickly picked up. He pointed it at Elena while Joe rushed to help Scott.

Just then, Katie cried out in pain. Joe knelt in front of Scott, reached over, grabbed Katie's hand, and picked up Scott's hand. He connected to both of them at the same time.

He blocked Scott from feeling what he felt, but didn't bother wasting his energy keeping Katie out. She could now simultaneously feel herself, Joe, Scott, and the baby. It was almost overwhelming.

Joe concentrated hard on helping Scott and Katie at the same time. He could feel that the bullet had entered Scott's liver, and he was bleeding internally. He instructed his body to push the bullet out of his liver, but not all the way out of his body. He wanted the doctors to believe the bullet stopped before damaging the liver. He then stopped all the bleeding before working on repairing the damage to his liver.

While doing that, he tried to slow Katie's labor. He could feel an increase in a particular hormone and assumed that was what triggered the labor. He told her body to stop the production of that hormone. He knew the production would start again once he disconnected from Katie, but it was the best he could do under the circumstances.

After a few minutes, they heard sirens. Joe let go of Scott's hand and stood up. He continued to hold Katie's hand but disconnected from her. He put his other hand in Katie's coat pocket and then looked at Larry, who was still holding Elena at gunpoint. He walked over to him, put something in his hand, and whispered in his ear. He then said in a normal voice, "Don't let her move."

He walked back to Katie and helped her walk out of the woods. They reached the road just as the first police car arrived. Two sheriff's deputies got out and asked if they were okay.

"My wife's in labor, and there are two gunshot victims in the woods there," he said, pointing. "We have the shooter subdued."

One of the officers said, "Hold tight. There are ambulances on the way."

The two officers rushed into the woods as an unmarked police car pulled in behind the patrol car. Detective Connor stepped out of her vehicle. She walked over to Katie and Joe, shook her head, and said, "I don't believe it. What are you two doing here?"

"The person who planted the bomb in Steve North's plane is out there," Katie said, motioning to the woods where the officers went. "She shot two people. Joe disarmed her. She's no longer a threat."

"They're both okay but need ambulances," Joe said. "Also, Katie is in labor. We need to get her to the hospital as soon as possible."

Connor returned to her vehicle and got on the radio. She gave the all-clear, and soon, two ambulances pulled up behind her car. She looked at Katie and Joe and said, "I'm afraid we're one ambulance short."

"Can you take us?" Joe asked.

Just then, Katie was hit with a contraction and winced in pain. Conner shook her head slowly and said, "Well, I guess the deputies can handle it from here. Do you think you can hold on until we get to the hospital?"

"Don't worry. She'll make it," Joe said.

***

As Katie and Joe got into the back seat, Connor got on the radio and informed headquarters about the situation and that she would be taking someone to the hospital. On the way, Joe connected to Katie and kept her contractions at bay. When they arrived at the hospital, Connor pulled up in front of the emergency room. She got out of the car and opened Katie's door. Joe got out, quickly walked around the car, and helped Katie get out.

Connor raced inside ahead of them. By the time Katie and Joe reached the door, a man with a wheelchair was standing near it. Katie sat in the chair. Connor said she needed to return to work but would check on her later.

"Do me a favor and call the resort," Joe said. "Let them know what is happening."

"I'll do that right away," Connor said.

They thanked her, and the man rolled Katie to the check-in area. Despite the emergency, they still needed to fill out paperwork. Katie looked at Joe and said, "Apparently, we wasted our time registering at that other hospital."

"It wasn't a waste," Joe said. "We helped a woman beat cancer."

Katie was about to say something, but was hit with another contraction. Joe looked at the intake woman and said, "Do you want to continue filling out paperwork while my wife gives birth right here, or can we finish this later?"

"We have the important stuff. We can finish the rest later." She wrote something on a piece of paper and waved to an orderly. She handed him the paper, and he pushed Katie to an elevator. He brought them to the Labor and Delivery Unit on the second floor.

A nurse put them in a room and helped prepare Katie for what was to come. While they waited, Katie asked, "What was it like when your other children were born?"

"I don't know. I had to wait outside."

"What? You mean you never saw the birth of any of your children?"

"It was a different time. Back then, birthing was a woman's domain, and men weren't welcome, except for the doctor, and more often than not, a midwife handled it."

"Did you have a doctor deliver your babies?"

"Yes, but we lived in the city at the time. Country folks often had to rely on a midwife."

Katie was hit with another contraction. As it subsided, a doctor walked in. He was older, of average build, and had thick, white hair. "Good afternoon, Mrs. Novak. I'm Dr. Pierce, and I'll be taking care of you today." He looked at Katie's chart and said, "It says here you have no primary doctor, nor do you have an obstetrician. Is that right?"

"That's right," Katie said.

"Okay. Don't worry. We'll take good care of you and your baby."

The doctor examined Katie and said, "Everything looks good. Your baby is fine. It shouldn't be long now. I'll be back shortly to check on you."

Two minutes later, Katie was hit with another contraction, worse than any before. "I think he's coming, Joe. I need you to do that pain reliever trick of yours."

Joe held Katie's hand and connected to her. He knew several hormones acted to reduce pain. Again, he didn't know their names but knew what each one did. He instructed her body to release enough of the hormones to reduce the pain, but not too much. He didn't want to diminish Katie's childbirth experience. He then hit the call button.

A nurse came in, and Joe told her it was time. She checked Katie and then picked up the phone and paged the doctor. When the doctor arrived, he examined Katie and said, "It's time."

Katie grabbed Joe's arm and whispered, "You know what I want."

Joe knew exactly what she wanted. She wanted to experience this childbirth from the inside. She wanted to feel what the baby was feeling. Joe was happy to do that for her because he also wanted to feel it. He connected to Katie just as the doctor told her to push.

Katie pushed, and the doctor said, "I see the head. One more good push will do it."

Katie pushed hard and felt the baby come out. It was painful, but also the most joyous feeling she had ever felt. The doctor picked up the baby and held him in one arm while he suctioned fluid from the baby's nose and mouth. Little Joey immediately started crying. The nurse cleaned him with a towel and then wrapped him. The doctor set the baby on Katie's abdomen while he checked him out.

Katie looked at him and cried. "He's the most beautiful thing I've ever seen."

The doctor clamped the umbilical cord and held up a pair of scissors. "Would you like to cut the cord?" he asked Joe.

"Really?" Joe asked. "I'd love to."

Joe took the scissors from the doctor and cut the cord. He smiled and handed the scissors back to the doctor. The nurse then put an identification tag on little Joey's wrist, and the doctor picked him up and put him on Katie's chest for her to hold. She put her arms around him and cried tears of joy.

After the doctor left, the nurse asked if she would like her to put the baby in the bassinet so Katie could get some rest. "No, not yet," Katie said. "Give me a little time."

"Of course," the nurse said before leaving.

"Would you like to hold him?" Katie asked Joe.

"I don't know. He's so little."

"You'll be fine. He's your son. You should hold him."

Joe gently picked up Joey and sat with him on a chair next to Katie. "He has so much hair," Joe said.

"He takes after his dad."

The door opened, and Michael and Susan came in. "We came as soon as we heard," Michael said. "I thought you were in West Bend."

"It's a long story," Joe said. "We'll fill you in later."

Susan walked around the bed to where Joe was sitting. "Oh my, he is so adorable," she said.

Joe stood up and said, "Would you like to hold him, Susan?"

"Do you even have to ask?" she said and held out her arms.

Joe handed Joey to Susan, who cradled him in her arms. "It's hard to believe this little guy is my brother."

They stayed and talked for another twenty minutes before Michael and Susan headed back to the resort. When they left, Joe gently placed a sleeping Joey into his bassinet. A couple of minutes later, a nurse came into the room, pushing a wheelchair with Sonia in it. She thanked the nurse, who promptly left.

Hi Sonia, Katie said. "How are you feeling?"

"I'm alive and well, thanks to you two again."

"How's Scott doing?" Joe asked.

"He'll be okay. The doctors think it's a miracle the bullet didn't damage his liver. They also think it's a miracle the bullet that hit me didn't do more damage than it did. I don't suppose you two know something about that?"

Katie looked at Joe and then back at Sonia. "What about you and Scott?"

"He just came out of surgery. It will be a little while before I can talk to him."

"What about your relationship? Do you see it ending?" she asked.

"That's hard to say. On the one hand, I am extremely angry and disappointed in him. On the other hand, he took a bullet to protect me."

"You have a tough choice to make," Joe said. "When trust is lost, it is hard to get it back. Although you should consider that Scott saw the error in his ways and called off the affair, which is what started all of this."

"I'm just going to take this one day at a time. I have a baby on the way, and that baby will need a father, whether we are together or not. Speaking of babies, how's your little guy doing?"

She rolled her chair close to the bassinet and said, "He is adorable. Was it a hard labor?"

"Don't worry," Katie said. "It's not easy, but it is so worth it."

"There was one other thing I wanted to mention," Sonia said. "When I was out there lying on the cold ground, I was certain I was going to die, but then an angel of God came to me. He held my hand, and I was one with him for a short time. I knew then that everything would be okay. Then he spoke. The voice I heard was Joe's voice."

"That was quite a dream," Joe said.

Sonia looked at Joe for a long moment. "Yeah, it was quite a dream."

Joe looked at Katie and then back at Sonia. "If you think that dream is something not worth mentioning to others, I'm sure I can help get your leg back to a hundred percent."

They spent the night at the hospital. Detective Conner returned to check on them. After she left, Eric arrived with his wife, Rachael, and their little girl. Rachael gave Katie plenty of advice on caring for an infant.

Chapter 15

The next morning, while Katie was lying on the bed holding little Joey, there was a knock at the door. Ashley came in, carrying a camera. She saw Katie and the baby and screamed with excitement. She set the camera down and hugged Katie. She stood up, hugged Joe, and then returned her attention to Joey. "He is so adorable," she said.

"Does Bob really want me to do this story looking like this?"

"Are you kidding? You just solved a crime and had a baby on the same day. This is exactly what you should look like."

Katie turned to Joe. "Do you want to hold Joey while I do this?"

"No," Ashly said. "I think our viewers would want to see both of you."

"Okay," Katie said. "Let's get this over with."

Ashly handed Katie a microphone before backing up to set up her shot. She positioned it so Joe was also in the frame. "Okay," she said. "Three... two... one..."

"Hello, Milwaukee. This is Katie Novak reporting for Channel 23 News. Much has happened these last few days, and I hope you forgive me for not looking my best. As you can see, my husband, Joe, and I welcomed the newest addition to our family yesterday. Meet Joseph Karl Novak.

"In other news, Joe and I witnessed the crash of a small airplane on Tuesday morning. Steven North, Founder and CEO of Zero North, a startup electric aircraft manufacturer in West Bend, was killed in the crash. Fortunately, his passenger, Sonia Wilson, survived.

"We soon discovered that someone had sabotaged the aircraft, and we were asked to investigate. During our investigation, we learned that a coworker, Elena Petrova, in an act of jealousy, set an explosive device on the aircraft to kill not Steven North but Sonia Wilson.

"Subsequently, she made another attempt to kill Sonia, shooting both her and her husband, Scott Wilson. Both are doing well and recovering in this hospital, while Elena Petrova is in police custody."

After Katie signed off, she handed the microphone back to Ashley. "I never imagined I would ever do a news report wearing a hospital gown."

"Life is full of surprises," Ashley said.

They talked for a while before Ashley had to get back to the station. As she was leaving, Katie's parents showed up. While they were there, Katie called Michael and arranged a room for them at the resort.

Not long after Katie's parents left, there was a knock at the door, and Larry and Max entered their room. They all greeted each other, and the two men paid some attention to little Joey before Larry took out an envelope and handed it to Katie.

"What's this?" she asked.

"It's payment for services. You proved that someone sabotaged our aircraft and identified the person responsible. You deserve it."

Katie opened the envelope and looked at the check. "This is too much."

"You saved Sonia's life. How much is that worth?"

"Yes, but you weren't able to prove to your client in time that your airplane works."

"We're not dead yet," Larry said. "Besides, that wasn't your fault. We are picking up the aircraft today. We arranged a truck to meet us there. We'll check everything out and try again once Sonia is well enough to travel. Hopefully, that will be soon."

"She'll be well enough quicker than you think," Joe said.

"I hope so," Larry said.

"I'm curious," Joe said, "how much money do you need to get you through until you are ready to deliver your first aircraft and get paid?"

"Oh, I don't know. Maybe another forty to fifty thousand dollars. That's assuming Sonia can get us the sale."

"Would you guys mind giving us two minutes alone?" Joe asked. "I want to ask Katie something?"

"Of course," Larry said before he and Max left the room and closed the door.

A couple of minutes later, Joe opened the door and motioned for them to return. Joe handed the check back to Larry. "We want to invest in your company. We can start with that. If you write up the paperwork, we'll wire you another fifty thousand dollars by tomorrow."

Larry looked shocked. "I don't believe it. That is very generous of you, but are you sure about this?"

"It's not generosity," Joe said. "After getting to know all of you, we are confident you will do well, and we will all make lots of money together."

"After getting to know you two, I'm pretty sure it's generosity, but I am in no position to refuse." Larry reached into his pocket and handed Joe a set of keys. "Here are your keys back."

Katie looked surprised and said, "Hey, those are my keys. Why did Larry have my keys?"

"I asked him to bring your car back from West Bend."

"Honey, you know how I feel about people driving my car."

"I know, that's why I didn't tell you." Joe looked at Larry. "Did you wreck her car on the way here?"

"Of course not. It's just like you left it, except I filled up the tank for you."

"Well, thank you, Larry and Max, for taking time out of your day to do that," Katie said.

"There is one other thing you might be interested in," Larry said. "The NTSB released its report this morning. They concluded someone sabotaged the aircraft."

I truly appreciate you taking the time to read Last Flight. I hope you enjoyed following Katie and Joe on their latest adventure.

I would be incredibly grateful if you left a review on Amazon, Goodreads, or wherever you purchased this book. Your thoughts help other readers discover the series and mean a lot to me as an author. Whether it's a few words or a detailed review, your feedback makes a difference.

Thank you again for your support. I couldn't do this without readers like you.

Charles Huss

Acknowledgment

I would like to express my deepest gratitude to Aisha Rajar for her beautiful illustrations, which grace the covers of every book in this series. She also gave Katie and Joe a face, which can be seen on the back cover of the printed edition of this book. In addition, she created stunning illustrations for my books Saving Apollo and Falling Star.

Books by Charles Huss

Last Healer Mysteries Series

Joe, a reclusive, ageless centenarian, meets Katie, an ambitious news personality with dreams of being an investigative reporter. Together, they solve crimes and explore the full potential of Joe's healing abilities while navigating the complexities of their intimate relationship.

The Last Healer

On the eve of her thirtieth birthday, Katie, a television news reporter, unhappy with her career and her love life, decides to spend the weekend alone at a Wisconsin ski resort.

Joe is a man content to live a private life in his cabin in the woods. Since the death of his wife, he has avoided intimate relationships and prefers to keep a low profile to prevent people from learning of his unusual abilities.

On the way to the ski resort, Katie makes a wrong turn during a snowstorm and hits Joe with her car. Lost and with no cell signal, Katie tries to keep Joe alive until she can get help. During Joe's recovery, Katie learns his secret and soon helps to investigate his family's mysterious past while Joe helps Katie investigate a double murder. Love blossoms while they slowly unravel both mysteries, but danger lies ahead. Can Joe discover the full extent of his abilities before it is too late?

Last Rites

In this gripping sequel to "The Last Healer," Katie and Joe, fresh from their honeymoon, must race to Milwaukee to save the life of Katie's dear friend Ashley after she and her mother fall victim to a ruthless attack. With Ashley on the brink of death, while a priest delivers Last Rites, her only chance for survival is Joe's remarkable healing powers.

What starts as a rescue mission turns into a murder investigation as they investigate the killing of Ashley's mother. While searching for the shooter, their investigation leads them to a chilling conspiracy centered on the city's homeless population. As they uncover more of the truth, they become targets as someone is determined to silence them. Will Katie and Joe find who is behind a series of murders, or will they become the next victims?

Last Chance

In Book Three of the Last Healer Mysteries, Katie and Joe, after deciding to quit investigating murders, are thrust back into it when a man is murdered at Joe's resort.

The victim is no ordinary man. He is a suspected jewel thief, believed to have hidden stolen jewels at the resort. While they struggle to handle all the treasure seekers, Katie and Joe debate how involved they should be in the murder investigation. They don't know the killer lurks in the background, taking orders from some of the most powerful people in Wisconsin while he waits for Katie and Joe to find what he is looking for.

Last Flight

In Book Four of the Last Healer Mysteries series, Katie and Joe witness the deadly crash of a prototype aircraft and save the life of one of its occupants. After Joe discovers evidence of sabotage, Katie insists she can investigate the crime despite being almost nine months pregnant.

Someone planted an explosive device in the aircraft, killing the company's founder and jeopardizing the struggling startup's future. Was the attack meant to destroy the company, or was it something more personal? As Katie and Joe hit one dead end after another, they discover the killer isn't finished. With time running out, they race to save the next victim, but with people dying, a murderer on the loose, and Katie in labor, what's a Healer to do?

Last Hope

In the fifth Last Healer Mystery, Katie and Joe learn of a tragedy in Katie's hometown while they are celebrating their son's first birthday. The husband of Katie's childhood best friend stands accused of murdering the community's lone police detective. They return to the small Wisconsin town, determined to find the real killer.

As they dig deeper, they uncover chilling ties between the detective's death and the recent killing of the mayor's daughter. It soon becomes clear someone will stop at nothing to keep the truth buried.

Other Books by Charles Huss

Truth Be Told

Peter Beckett awoke 25 years ago with no memory of his past. Since then, he's been haunted by a gift he never asked for and doesn't want. People can't lie to him. To Peter, it feels like a curse that has left him isolated and feared by all who get to know him. Only his priest accepts him for who he is.

The FBI has been watching him, and they need his unique talent to track a deadly drug cartel that has infiltrated Milwaukee, fueling a dangerous spike of fentanyl overdoses. Rookie agent Hannah Meyers is assigned to recruit Peter, who is reluctant to help, but is intrigued by Hannah after she lies to him.

As the investigation deepens, details of Peter's former life emerge. With secrets unraveling and lives on the line, Peter must decide whether to return to the glorious life he once knew or give it all up for love.

Saving Apollo

Apollo is no ordinary dog. Along with his sister, Athena, he was genetically modified to be smarter than a chimpanzee. When the lead geneticist quits over a dispute about the fate of the dogs, chaos erupts, and Apollo escapes, ending up on a small island off the Florida coast. There, he befriends twelve-year-old Ethan, who has just moved to the island with his dad, Ryan.

As they uncover Apollo's extraordinary ability to understand them, they also learn about the perilous fate that awaits him if he returns. With the help of their neighbor, Brooke, a local veterinarian, they devise a plan to save Apollo and Athena. Standing in their way is Jack Strauss, a former Marine and head of security at the lab that created Apollo and Athena.

"Saving Apollo" is a heartwarming, family-friendly story of friendship, love, and compassion.

Falling Star

A meteorite crashes into the serene wilderness of a national park. In its aftermath, both people and animals succumb to aggressive behavior followed by death. Two rookies, FBI agent Beth Hartley and Park Ranger Mike Bauer, are put together to investigate the strange events.

Beth is tough as they come on the outside but vulnerable on the inside. After her last breakup, she has given up on men to focus on her career. Mike, a former military police officer, has developed trust issues and prefers his new career where he has no partner that he needs to rely on.

As their investigation brings them closer to the truth, they find themselves getting closer to each other. In a dangerous forest where every animal is a potential threat, and even the air could be toxic, their best chance for survival is a partner they can trust.

Identity Crisis

After Alex Neumann agrees to participate in his father's groundbreaking memory recording experiment, he awakens years later to find he is not the man he used to be. He soon becomes a pawn in a deadly scheme involving a ruthless businessman, an Army general, and the President of The United States.

As Alex peels away layers of deception, his true identity slowly emerges, along with skills foreign to his old self. He will need all those skills and the help of friends he meets along the way to survive and turn the tables on his adversaries.

Bad Cat Chris: The Baddest Cat You'll Ever Love

When Chuck volunteered to help a local cat shelter clean cages one morning, the last thing he expected was a kitten climbing up his back to perch on his shoulders, but that was the beginning of a relationship that would test the limits of human endurance and compassion.

This is the story of Chris, a cat like no other who would turn the lives of Chuck and Rose upside-down while eventually showing them that bad can be good and love can come from the most unlikely places.

This book is based on Chris's blog at BadCatChris.com and is a collection of sometimes serious but mostly humorous stories about the ups and downs of living with a bad cat.

About The Author

Charles Huss was born and raised in the suburbs of Chicago but has lived most of his adult life in the Tampa Bay, Florida, area. He is a graduate of St. Petersburg College and the author of several books. He currently lives with his wife, Rose, and their two cats.

Don't miss out!

Visit the website below and you can sign up to receive emails whenever Charles Huss publishes a new book. There's no charge and no obligation.

https://books2read.com/r/B-A-LHRY-ZGTAG

BOOKS 2 READ

Connecting independent readers to independent writers.

Did you love *Last Flight*? Then you should read *Last Hope*[1] by Charles Huss!

In the fifth Last Healer Mystery, Katie and Joe learn of a tragedy in Katie's hometown while they are celebrating their son's first birthday. The husband of Katie's childhood best friend stands accused of murdering the community's lone police detective. They return to the small Wisconsin town, determined to find the real killer.As they dig deeper, they uncover chilling ties between the detective's death and the recent killing of the mayor's daughter. It soon becomes clear someone will stop at nothing to keep the truth buried.

Read more at charleshuss.com.

---

1. https://books2read.com/u/3yjY2L

2. https://books2read.com/u/3yjY2L

www.ingramcontent.com/pod-product-compliance
Lightning Source LLC
Chambersburg PA
CBHW031427200626
46814CB00016B/2817